She wa

when a car pul [BARCODE] ___ out, blocking her way to the hotel. What? She turned and ran. His footsteps pounded after her, closing the distance. She shouted, "*Au secours*! Help! Police!" The street was empty of pedestrians. Rough hands seized her from behind in a fierce grip. She tried to scream but his hand covered her mouth brutally, grinding her lips across her teeth, covering her nose, making it difficult to breathe. His other arm came around her waist and he pulled her backwards, toward the waiting car. Her heart pounded as she struggled in his fierce grip.

"Bitch," he said, "you want to live, you cooperate."

Caitlin forced herself to go limp, as if she had fainted, her lead lolling, her arms dangling at her sides. His grasp loosened as he half dragged, half carried, her dead weight toward the car. More focused on keeping her upright than on keeping her restrained, his grip on her slackened. Caitlin twisted her body out of his embrace, and using the side of her hand to deliver a sharp blow to the base of his nose, she shoved her knee into his groin. He grunted and doubled over in pain, his nose gushing blood. She broke loose and ran toward the busy intersection, where she could see people, find help.

Too late. They were on her again, the two men she had last seen in Berkeley.

Praise for Blair McDowell

"Like all of Blair McDowell's marvelous books, *FATAL CHARM* is a non-stop romantic suspense thrill ride from beginning to end. If you love well-crafted romantic suspense where the mystery is every bit as mysterious as the romance is romantic, check out Blair McDowell's work."

~ Marlene, Reading Reality

~*~

"A worthy successor to *WHERE LEMONS BLOOM*. This time romance and intrigue moves from the Amalfi Coast to the City of Love and does not disappoint!"

~Heather, Eyes.2c

~*~

"Well-written and engaging. I have read all of Blair McDowell's books and, for me, *FATAL CHARM* tops the charts. I look forward to reading Ms. McDowell's future works."

~Kristina Anderson

~*~

"The writing and craftsmanship is delicate and intricately beautiful...deserves to be a top shelf read."

~Aanandite Maitra, Reading Alley

~*~

"A heartwarming, perceptive romance with just enough high-stakes drama to keep readers turning the pages."

~Kirkus Reviews

~*~

"Blair McDowell's writing abilities are the best I've come across yet."

~Sherman Morrison

Fatal Charm

by

Blair McDowell

Blair McDowell

Fatal Charm

Cover Art by *Tina Lynn Stout*

The Wild Rose Press, Inc.
PO Box 708
Adams Basin, NY 14410-0708
Visit us at www.thewildrosepress.com

Publishing History
First Crimson Rose Edition, 2017
Print ISBN 978-1-5092-1617-8
Digital ISBN 978-1-5092-1618-5

Published in the United States of America

A note from the author

The jeweled dragon on which this story is based is a figment of my imagination. In my research for *Fatal Charm*, involving numerous trips to the Louvre in Paris, I discovered no jewels from the Louis XVI monarchy have survived except the Regent Diamond. It was said once to have adorned Marie Antoinette's hat. Over the years there have been several thefts from the Louvre, some from the jewelry collection, so the premise of *Fatal Charm* lies within the realm of possibility.

After Paris, I chose Concarneau in Brittany as my setting, because it is an interesting and unique part of France but also because it was the setting of a novel by Georges Simenon, *The Yellow Dog*. Concarneau has changed little in the more than half century since that classic detective story was written, except that the famous blue fishing nets are now brought out only on festive occasions.

Several people assisted me in the research for *Fatal Charm*. I thank Wendy Walsh, for sharing her knowledge about jewelry design and creation, Gay Soetekouw, for her intimate knowledge of Paris, Alain Lane for helping me with some impolite French phrases, Mark Panagapka for sharing his understanding of paramedic procedures, Sherry Royal for her help in marketing, and Jeanette Panagapka, for being, as always, my tireless traveling companion and fearless driver.

Most of all, I thank my editor, Kinan Werdski, whose patience, help and suggestions made *Fatal Charm* a much better book.

Chapter One

He watched, hypnotized, as the stream of blood snaked its way down his arm, soaking the sleeve of his torn shirt, dripping on the floor, slowly dripping his life away. With the last of his strength, he struggled against the duct tape binding his arms and legs, keeping him imprisoned in the heavy chair. No use. His mouth was dry, he could hardly swallow, probably the effect of the drug they injected him with. What had he told them under the influence of that drug?

His vision blurred and his head dropped to his chest. He jerked it up again, willing himself not to lose consciousness. Not yet. He had to warn Caitlin. He had to get a message to her. She was in grave danger as long as the dragon was in her possession. And she didn't even know she had it. How could he have placed her in such peril? He cared for Caitlin. She didn't deserve this.

He laughed a small bitter laugh. He could do nothing. Nothing for her, nothing for himself. His head nodded again. This time he couldn't summon the strength to raise it. There was a persistent ringing in his ears.

The acrid smell of smoke roused him from his stupor. Bastards. They'd set fire to the building. They were leaving nothing to chance. No matter. Nothing mattered any more. He had been incredibly stupid and he was paying for his stupidity with his life. But Cait... not Caitlin, he prayed, as he slipped into oblivion.

****

Five minutes later the fire department arrived, sirens wailing, and moments after, an ax crashed through the locked door.

"Christ! There's a man in here! Cut him loose and get him out of here. This whole building's going to go any minute."

The first firefighter cut quickly through the restraints while the second hoisted the unconscious man over his shoulder and they raced into the smoke filled hallway, down the stairs and out through the front door.

Outside, the paramedics took over. "What happened here?"

"Don't know. We found him unconscious, trussed up like a Christmas turkey. Somebody wanted him to go up with the building."

Together, the paramedics lifted him onto the stretcher. "Keep him upright. He's having trouble breathing. Try to staunch the bleeding while I get him on oxygen!"

"I'm trying. Looks like multiple knife wounds. We'd better get him to Berkeley General fast. His pulse rate isn't good and his blood pressure's dropping."

Suddenly the patient opened his eyes wide, pulled the oxygen mask down and grasped the paramedic's arm, struggling to say something.

"What? What did you say?"

"Must warn Cait—Warn—the am—let!" The hand dropped.

"I'm not getting a pulse here!"

****

2

Caitlin Abernathy woke to a foggy morning in the Berkeley hills. She shrugged. The fog would burn off by noon. It always did.

She headed for the bathroom. As she lathered shampoo through her thick dark hair, she thought back to Allen's hot, demanding kisses the night before with a smile of remembered pleasure. Then her smile turned to a frown as she recalled their argument over dinner.

"I don't see what the problem is," he'd reasoned. "We've been seeing each other for months now. Why won't you sleep with me? I know you want to. Why do you keep pushing me away? Why can't I move in with you? It's ridiculous for us to be paying for two places when I could be helping you with your mortgage here."

It had been difficult to answer him. From a strictly financial view, what he suggested made sense, but she just couldn't. While his kisses sometimes made her want more, hers was a purely physical response. Her heart and mind weren't engaged. She wanted something more, something she couldn't quite define.

In the end she had opted for some small part of the truth. "I'm sorry, Allen, I'm not ready for that kind of commitment."

She couldn't bring herself to tell him she didn't love him. She'd slipped without much thought into the relationship. In retrospect, she suspected she hadn't been fair to him. He loved her, or at least he said he did, but, although she was fond of Allen—

"I just can't," she'd told him with more than a little regret. Had she been wrong? She had held him at a distance, not sure whether she wanted to take the next, natural step of letting him make love to her, move in with her. He was a thoroughly nice man. A bit dull and predictable, but dependable. They could probably build a good life together. Maybe that was all there was.

She smiled, remembering their meeting four months ago. She'd been delivering to a jewelry shop on the Embarcadero where the owner always carried a few of her best pieces. It had taken longer than she'd anticipated and she was rushing back to her car, hoping to get to the parking meter before the meter maid did. In her hurry she'd run full tilt into Allen, knocking him down and scattering the parcels he was carrying all over the sidewalk.

Flustered and embarrassed, she'd apologized profusely. He'd picked himself up, laughing, and suggested the only adequate apology would be for her to have lunch with him. He had a wonderful, winning laugh. It was his laugh that made her say yes.

They went together to feed her meter, and then picnicked on a baguette and cheese and drank good French wine in the park overlooking the sailboat harbor and the Golden Gate Bridge. That had been the beginning.

Caitlin liked being with Allen. He had an infectious gaiety. He never failed to lift her spirits when she was down. And until last night their relationship had been a lighthearted friendship with no strings attached on either side. What had changed? Why was he suddenly so insistent on moving in with her?

Oh, well, she'd think about that later. Right now, she had more important things to think about. Like her upcoming meeting with the buyer from the mega-luxury store, Marcus-Pfeiffer. What was she going to wear for her very important appointment with him this morning?

She stepped out of the shower and rubbed the terry towel through her tangled hair and down her body. After using the blow dryer briefly, she ran her fingers through her almost dry hair. Trying to restore the wanton curls to some semblance of order, she pulled them ruthlessly back into the sophisticated twist she always wore for business, securing it with curved combs. A few unruly tendrils curled around her face. She always wore her hair up to display the earrings and necklaces she created. If she could get this contract for her jewelry designs from Marcus-Pfeiffer, it would be a major coup. Not to mention money in the bank. She could pay off her mortgage years sooner with the money they promised.

Her mind veered briefly to Allen's suggestion about living together, to his offer of help with her mortgage. Much as she wanted to be debt free, she suspected drifting into a committed relationship without love wasn't the best way to go about it. She wasn't sure she believed in fairy tales or happily ever after, but she wasn't ready to settle for less, just yet.

Slipping into a black lace bikini and matching bra, Caitlin pushed through her skimpy closet and selected a simple black linen dress. It would frame very nicely the blood red of the mookite necklace she had just finished yesterday. The short tube sheathed her body, hinting at rather than displaying her curves. She touched her eyelids with shadow matching the amber of her eyes, and added a slash of crimson lipstick. Then she fastened the large chunky red and gold necklace around her neck and put the matching bracelet on her right arm. Stepping back, she surveyed the effect in her full-length mirror. It would do, she thought, as she slipped her feet into her old but elegant black Ferragamo's with four-inch heels. She picked up her purse and headed for the door. No time for breakfast. She'd grab a coffee at the Starbucks next to her shop when she stopped there to pick up her sample case.

She pulled her five-year-old Toyota out of its curbside parking place. Absently tapping her fingers in time to WQXR on her car radio, Caitlin navigated the steep Berkeley hills to the center of town, encountering increasing traffic as she approached the area around the university. How fortunate she was to have a shop on College Avenue. It wasn't easy to find affordable commercial space in this part of town. She even had a miniscule parking slot at the back of the building.

Letting herself into the back door with her key, Caitlin turned off the alarm and walked into her workshop. It occupied most of the ground floor in the narrow two-story building.

She switched on the bright light suspended over her high worktable. Fingering the piece she was currently working on, a small gold frog sitting on a jade lily pad, she frowned. What stones should she use for his eyes? She walked over to the wall of cabinets where she kept her stones. They were stored in old-fashioned oak filing cabinets, the kind libraries used to have before everything was computerized. She smiled as she remembered her good fortune in acquiring these cabinets. She'd bid on them in an auction when she was first setting up her business, and was astonished at her good luck when nobody else wanted them and her very modest bid made them hers. Their small deep drawers were perfect for storing all her gemstones. She had them organized alphabetically, just as the original library cards used to be. Abalone and aquamarine to tourmaline and zirconia; thirty-two kinds of semi-precious stones. They represented a major investment, one she could never have made without the help of the bank.

She frowned, thinking about the size of the mortgage she had taken on the house her parents had left her, to buy this small, rather dilapidated two-story building on College Avenue. Someday, maybe she'd be able to pay it off.

The frog. What stone would look best? Absently Caitlin opened the moonstone drawer. They might work, although perhaps something brighter would be better. She opened another drawer and fingered through the turquoise. She knew her stones as much by their feel as by the way they looked. No. Not the turquoise. They were a bit too obvious. Perhaps obsidian?

She heard someone at the front door and pushed the drawer closed. She walked through to the salesroom, with its three glass cases displaying her original jewelry designs. A very tall black man with dreadlocks half way to his waist, sporting wire-framed glasses and wearing a multicolored shirt, a leather vest, and black velvet cords, was letting himself in the College Avenue entrance with his key.

He pushed his bicycle past her into the back room. "Sorry I'm late, Cait. Professor Humbolt's eight o'clock class ran a little over. I know you got big doings over in Frisco this morning. But I'm here now. You better get going."

"Thanks, Aristotle. Mrs. Cummings will be coming later this morning to pick up the lemon quartz bracelet she ordered. The price is two hundred fifty. Don't let her give you any grief on the amount. She agreed to it when she ordered the piece."

"No problem, Cait. Go on now. Git!"

"I just stopped by to pack my sample case."

Caitlin went back into her workroom and selected some finished pieces she thought might interest the buyer from the mega-luxury store. The tiger-eye pendant, the lacy collar made of carnelian and moonstone. The delicate lemon quartz necklace and matching bracelet. A few of her best, most expensive pieces. Not too many. Each one unique, each a one-of-a-kind piece. She'd found customers would pay well for designs they knew they'd never see on anyone else.

Picking up her case, she called, "I'm leaving now, Aristotle." Car keys in hand, Caitlin went out the back door.

A dark sedan was blocking her exit from the parking lot. Annoyed, she went over and rapped on the car window.

"Could you please move? I need to get out."

Before the words were out of her mouth two men leaped out of the car, pushing her against it, hemming her in. Something jabbed into her ribs. She glanced down and gasped. A gun. It was a gun.

Caitlin shivered. "What do you want?"

Their eyes were bleak, expressionless. Her mind registered they were both very well dressed. They had on suits and ties, for God's sake. Somehow, the way they were dressed made them more intimidating. Nobody wore suits and ties in Berkeley.

"The case. We'll take the case. Just put it down and you won't get hurt."

Caitlin's chin went up as she pulled her case

against her, holding it tight with both arms. "I will not give you my case. I need it to show to a buyer. Why on earth would you want to steal my case? I work in semi-precious stones, not diamonds and emeralds. There's nothing of great value in my case. It's certainly not worth armed robbery."

"*Putain*, you talk too much!" The taller man wrenched the case out of her arms and shoved Caitlin roughly.

Off balance, she fell. Before she could get to her feet again the two were back in the car, speeding down the alley.

"Damn." Caitlin brushed herself off. She inspected her dress and shoes. Still presentable. Her leg was scraped and she had turned her ankle in the fall. She limped back into the shop.

Aristotle looked up, his eyebrows raised in surprise, when she hobbled into the showroom. "What happened? You fell down?" He took her arm and led her to a chair. "Sit down. Your leg looks nasty. Let me wash it off."

Now that it was over, Caitlin was shaking. Aristotle disappeared into the bathroom adjoining her workshop and was back a moment later with a basin of warm water and a cloth. He set about looking after the scrape on Caitlin's leg with a care that might have surprised anyone but Caitlin. She knew from her five years of working with this fierce-looking giant he was capable of great gentleness.

"You gonna tell me what happened? You didn't just fall down. Although in those heels I don't know why not."

"Two men…knocked me down and took my case."

"What! Did you get a good look at them?"

"I most certainly did. They were dressed like they were going to a funeral. I thought for a minute it might be mine. The tall one had a gun pressed into my side. He was skinny, almost skeletal. The other one was short and dumpy. They both looked, I don't know, really scary. Like they'd as soon kill you as look at you."

Caitlin clasped her hands together tightly, trying to still their shaking. "The tall man spoke with an accent, but I couldn't place it. He called me *putain*. What's that? It didn't sound nice."

Aristotle took her two slender hands in his very large ones and rubbed them. "It's French, and no, it's not nice. But it's okay, Caitlin, you're safe now. Just breathe. Take a deep breath and let it out slowly."

"But my case!" she cried. "They drove off with my sample case. What am I going to do about the buyer from Marcus-Pfeiffer?"

Aristotle pulled out his large red handkerchief and dried her eyes. "You've smudged your makeup. You've got lots of other good pieces you can show him. Show him the ones you're wearing. They're gorgeous." His brow creased. "But why would anybody bother to steal your sample case? The stones take most of their value from the way you've set them. I suppose they could melt down the settings for the silver and gold, but it seems a lot of work for a small return."

"I don't know. I told them the pieces wouldn't have much resale value. They didn't seem to care."

"We've got to call the police."

"Not now. If I have to wait for them I'll miss my appointment."

"How's the leg? The ankle?"

Caitlin stood and flexed her foot. "They seem to be okay."

"Then go fix your face and choose a few other pieces to show your buyer while I call Mrs. Cummings to change her appointment. Then I'll lock up the place."

"Why?"

"You don't think I'm gonna let you drive into San Francisco by yourself after this? Look at your hands. They're still shaking. Besides, if you're driving you'll have to find a parking space and you'll be late for your appointment. I'll drop you off in front of the Mark Hopkins Hotel and go park the car. I'll meet you in the lobby when you're through."

"But my case is gone," Caitlin wailed.

Aristotle shook his head. "Put the pieces in one of those fancy bags you were so hot to buy for the shop. Probably better anyway. They have your name on them."

****

Two hours later Caitlin emerged from the elevator and walked across to where Aristotle was waiting for her, sitting in one of the comfortable sofas in the lobby of the hotel.

"Don't tell me. I can see by your smile he liked them."

Caitlin beamed at him. "The store's going to take twenty pieces right away. If those sell well, they'll take another thirty for their Christmas catalogue. I'm going to have to work hard to supply as many pieces as they want."

"Congratulations. You've earned this."

****

Back at the shop Caitlin surveyed her now depleted

11

show cases. "I'll have to work day and night if I'm to meet the deadlines for the Christmas catalog. Their buyer took all the pieces I had with me, even the ones I was wearing. And I'll have to make some new ones immediately for our display cases. I can't afford to let my bread and butter business slip."

"Anything I can do to help?"

"No. Just man the shop. I'll be in my workroom."

"We really should call the police, you know."

Two uniformed officers opened the door and walked into the showroom. "Ms. Abernathy?"

Aristotle and Caitlin stared at the officers. "How did you know to come?" Caitlin asked. "We hadn't called you yet. Who reported the theft?"

"Theft?" The officers looked confused. The older one took charge. "I'm Detective O'Malley and this is Officer Thurgood. Are you Caitlin Abernathy?"

"Yes."

"You know a man named Allen Thompson?"

"Yes, I know Allen. Why do you want to know?"

The officers looked pained. "Maybe you should sit down, Miss," Officer Thurgood suggested.

Caitlin looked from one to the other of the men and drew herself up to her full five foot eight inches. "I'll remain standing. Tell me about Allen. Has he been in an accident? Is he hurt? Where is he?"

"I'm sorry to have to tell you, ma'am, but Allen Thompson is dead."

The blood drained from Caitlin's head and her legs gave way. Aristotle caught her as she fainted. When she came to, she was on the bench in her workroom with Aristotle hovering over her. The two policemen were still there.

"I'm sorry we had to inform you of his death this way," the older officer said. "But we hoped perhaps you could shed some light on the matter. Do you know his whereabouts last night?"

She looked, puzzled, into their faces. "He was with me. How did he die? Was he in an automobile accident?"

"What time did you last see him?" the officer spoke gently.

Tears streaked down her cheeks. Allen. Dear, sweet, funny Allen. Gone? How could it be? He had been an increasing part of her life for... She brought her mind back to the two policemen standing before her. What weren't they telling her?

"Did he have an accident on the way home?" she asked again.

The detective persisted. "What time was it when he left? Did he say where he was going?"

"Around eleven. He always left around eleven. And I naturally assumed he was going home to his apartment in Oakland."

"I see. So you've been in an intimate relationship with Allen Thompson for...?"

Caitlin's chin went up. "We were not in an *intimate* relationship. We were just friends."

"And you have no idea who he might have been going to meet when he left you?"

"Going to meet? No. I assumed he went home to his own place in Oakland. We'd been talking about moving in together but..." Frowning, Caitlin looked up at the two officers. "What aren't you telling me? What happened? How did Allen die?"

Detective O'Malley gave her a piercing look. "We

have reason to believe Allen Thompson was murdered."

"Murdered? No, it's not possible." Caitlin's voice shook. "Who would do such a thing? And why? Allen had no enemies." Her shoulders slumped as she gave in to the weeping threatening for the past several minutes.

The detective continued, "We found your name and number on his iPhone. The paramedics said he died with your name on his lips. He was trying to warn you of some danger. I believe his last words were, "Must warn Caitlin...the omelet..." Does that make any sense to you?"

"The omelet?" Caitlin looked up at the two men through her tears. "It makes no sense at all. Allen didn't even like omelets. I never made an omelet for him. Could he have been delirious?"

"Perhaps."

"You still haven't told me how he died."

"We're waiting for the autopsy report, but his death appears to have been from a combination of blood loss and smoke inhalation. He was left, injured and restrained, in an old warehouse that was then set on fire."

"My God! Allen? Who would do such a thing?" She hiccupped through her tears.

Aristotle brought her a glass of water. "Drink."

Caitlin sipped. The hiccups subsided.

Officer Thurgood waited until he had her attention. "We're looking at murder and arson so you can see why we're interested in discovering his movements last evening."

"After he left me?" She sniffed and Aristotle handed her his red kerchief. "What can I say? As far as I know, he always went home. He is...was...serious

14

about getting eight hours sleep. He always left me by eleven."

"Did Allen Thompson have any connections of which you're aware with criminal elements? Did he use recreational drugs?"

In spite of the circumstances, Caitlin gave a small laugh. "Allen? Don't be absurd! Allen was an accountant. He was the most conventional man I've ever known. He was very nice, but he was..." Caitlin searched for the right word. Dull seemed unkind. "Predictable," she said. "A creature of habit. He didn't smoke, he didn't drink, except for a little wine with dinner. He was a thoroughly nice man."

"Well, your thoroughly nice man got himself mixed up in something that led to his murder. And when we searched his apartment earlier today, we found it had been trashed. Somebody is looking for something Allen Thompson had. Are you sure you don't know what it might be?"

Caitlin shook her head, baffled. "I have no idea."

"With his dying breath he asked the paramedics to warn you. I think you'd better take the warning seriously." The detective shook his head. "If you think of anything you haven't told us, give us a call." He handed her a card.

The two officers were at the door when the younger one turned back and said, "When we came in you said something about a theft? What were you talking about?"

Aristotle answered. "Caitlin was knocked down this morning right in our parking lot. Two guys threatened her with a gun and snatched her sample case. She was on her way to San Francisco to meet with a buyer."

The officers came back inside. "The case had jewelry in it?" Officer Thurgood pointed to the showcase. "Like the stuff in here?"

"Yes." Caitlin straightened her back and looked at the few remaining pieces.

"How valuable are they?"

Caitlin walked over, took a piece out of the case, and held it up to the light. "They range in price from thirty-five dollars for a simple setting like this onyx and silver pin"—she replaced the pin and picked up a filigreed gold necklace set with a dozen small amethysts—"to about four hundred fifty for a piece like this."

The two policemen leaned forward to study the pieces in the display cabinets.

Aristotle added, "Caitlin has a feel for how to combine stones and how to use gold or silver, or sometimes even copper to enhance the stones in her designs."

"Hmm. And you would be…?"

"Aristotle Jones. I'm Caitlin's assistant. Have been for five years."

"Aristotle is a doctoral student in history at UC Berkeley," Caitlin explained. "He lives over the shop."

Aristotle frowned. "It's hard to see how this morning's theft could have anything to do with Allen Thompson's death."

Detective O'Malley shook his head. "At this point, we don't know what's related and what isn't. We'll send someone from the robbery division around to take down the particulars. Meanwhile, I suggest you take some simple precautions, Ms. Abernathy."

Chapter Two

The weeks followed in a blur for Caitlin. The police asked her to identify the body, a horrible experience that gave her nightmares. They returned twice to question her, but she could add little to what she'd originally said. Then they asked her to come to the station to look through mug shots to see if she could identify the two men who had accosted her. When she couldn't, they had her work with a police artist to create a likeness of the two, saying the theft might possibly have some connection to Allen Thompson's death. The police artist had come up with very good images of the two men, but as far as she knew, they had not yet identified them.

The more questions the police asked, the more Caitlin realized how little she knew about Allen Thompson. She didn't know where he came from, whether he had family, where he had gone to school, or even where he worked. All the minutiae that made up a life. She'd commented once on his slight but charming accent, and he told her he'd grown up in Quebec, but he never elaborated. Looking back, Caitlin realized he seldom volunteered any information on his past.

Late in March the police released Allen's body for burial. It was Caitlin who made the funeral arrangements. There was no one else to do so.

On a chilly, damp morning, she stood at Allen's

graveside, beside Aristotle, numb, unable to feel anything other than emptiness. She brought spring flowers from her garden, daffodils and lilacs. She had always loved the scent of lilacs, but for some reason, they made her slightly nauseated this morning. The world was painted in tones of gray. Pines and live oaks scattered throughout the cemetery seemed almost ominous, dark and dripping from the night's heavy rainfall.

They were the only two mourners present, although she had put a notice of the funeral in the San Francisco and Oakland papers. Had he no family? No colleagues at work who cared? The police had been unable to trace any, and he'd rarely spoken of his past. She knew so little about him. But Allen had mattered to her. She'd miss the comfort of his presence. He'd made a place for himself in her heart. While she'd never been in love with him, she'd cared about him. He'd been a good friend.

The priest was intoning the last words of the Catholic burial service. She knew Allen was Catholic because of the St. Christopher medal he always wore around his neck on a gold chain. When she asked him about it, he told her it had been his father's, he'd been raised Catholic and at one time had even been an altar boy. Looking back, she realized it was the only time he'd ever confided anything about his life before they met.

Her mind swerved to the manner of his death. What on earth could Allen, stable, ordinary Allen, have been involved in? It wasn't drugs. He didn't smoke anything. He'd been horrified when he once found a joint in a drawer in Caitlin's living room table. He made her promise never again to do drugs of any kind. It was a promise she could make easily. She never had used drugs of any kind. The joint had been left there by a man she dated briefly before Allen. She'd just neglected to throw it away.

Aristotle put his arm around her, pulling her close, and handed her his large red handkerchief, wordlessly comforting her.

Finally the short service was over. As they turned away from the grave, Aristotle said, "Home?"

"No. I think I'd like to work for a while. It helps me get my mind focused. Let's go to the shop. But you're free once we get there. I won't open up. I'll work on the order for Marcus-Pfeiffer."

"Good. I've got a paper to work on for my class in anthropology. I'll be right upstairs if you need me."

Caitlin sighed. "Should I have let him move in, maybe even married him, Aristotle? I keep thinking if I had married him, maybe…"

"No, you shouldn't have married him. There was no karma between you. Tell you the truth, Cait, I was really worried you might. It would have been bad news for both of you. It wasn't just you it was wrong for."

"Thanks, Aristotle. I know you're right. But I can't help thinking if I'd been more in his life, known more about him, this might not have happened."

****

Back in the familiar, comforting space of her workshop, Caitlin soon lost herself in her craft. She finished the little frog and began making sketches for a krynite pendant with matching earrings. She'd set them in silver. It would set off the silvery blue of the stones.

She was deeply involved in her work when the bell

in the shop rang. Had Aristotle forgotten to put the "Closed" sign on the door?

She stood and stretched. Her back muscles were cramped from hovering over her worktable. She'd been at it for six hours. She needed a break. She went through to the shop and opened the door just as the man rang the bell again.

"The sign says to ring the bell." His voice was low, melodious, with just a trace of a lilt.

"It should have been turned to the 'Closed' side, but since you're here, come in."

She looked up into the bluest eyes she'd ever seen. Dark blue, like a midnight sky. Surrounded by dense black lashes. He was tall. Almost as tall as Aristotle.

"Come in," she repeated, stepping back.

He followed her into the showroom, looked around for a moment, then peered into her glass display case. "I need a birthday present for my mother. Something special, it's her sixtieth. A friend recommended you."

"I'm sorry. I don't have much left to show. But if you have the time, I could make something for you."

"I'd have no idea how to go about that. When I see a finished piece I can generally tell whether it's something she'd like, but…"

"Tell me about her. How tall is she? What color hair and eyes? Does she like casual clothes or is she into high fashion? What's her favorite color?"

"Oh, I see. You fit the jewelry to the person. What a clever idea. Let's see…" His gaze raked her from head to toe.

"She's about your height. Not as slender as you. Has anyone ever told you you look like a dancer? That long neck and those long, long legs?"

Catlin blushed under his scrutiny and was furious at herself for her uncontrolled reaction to his words. She spoke more sharply than she intended to. "It's your mother we're supposed to be talking about, not me," she snapped. She looked into his bland expression and saw his lips twitch with a suppressed smile.

"Her colorin'?" he continued as is she hadn't spoken. "Pretty much the same as mine, blue eyes, red hair. It's the Celtic curse. We've all had the same colorin' for generations in my family."

Caitlin studied him. Red was not what she'd have called it. Molten gold. The kind of hair the sun god, Apollo, might have had. It was carelessly combed and looked like it hadn't seen a barber in recent history. It curled over the collar of his tweed jacket. To complete the sun god image, he sported a neatly trimmed beard. His face could have come off an ancient gold coin.

She thought for a few moments. "Amber," she said. "Amber is a beautiful color on redheads. Let me show you some. If you see a piece you like, I can sketch up some possible designs for you." She looked up and down her customer, assessing his ability to pay. Lord, he was tall. Certainly over six feet. And very well built. Broad shoulders, slim waist. He must work out. His clothes were of good quality, but his jacket had a rather slept-in look. He seemed, what...? Careless of his appearance? But he was very attractive.

"Amber?" he said, bringing her back to the business at hand. He smiled and Caitlin had the uncanny sense he knew exactly what she had been thinking.

"Come into my workshop," she invited, leading him through the door to the back of the shop.

She went to her drawers. Amber was close to the top of the far left cabinet, just below abalone. She pulled out the drawer and carried it over to her worktable. She looked into the drawer and selected pieces ranging in size from very small to about an inch in diameter.

The man studied each piece turning it over in his hands, bringing it under the light. "These are very nice." He looked at her intently. "They're the color of your eyes. They'd look great on you…"

Uncomfortable under his scrutiny, Caitlin fidgeted with the stones in the drawer. The "r" in his *very* and *great* sort of trilled. Not quite a rolled "r" like in Italian or Spanish, more like a sort of tripping over the sound. Scottish? Irish?

"… but I think somehow they'd not be what she'd choose. Blue. She likes blue."

"Lapis." Caitlin scooped up the amber and returned the drawer to the cabinet before she moved down to the fourth cabinet, the L's.

She took the drawer out and carefully set several of the deep blue stones on her table.

"Aye. This is more to her taste. He picked up each stone and turned it this way and that, under the light. "This one," he said, choosing a large, almost oval piece. "I think she'd like this one."

Caitlin looked at the stone he'd chosen. It was one of the most expensive pieces in her shop. She wondered if he could afford it. She'd better let him know up front what the cost might be.

"The stone you've chosen is a hundred and fifty dollars, and with a custom setting in silver it would run another hundred fifty. Are you sure you don't want something smaller?"

"I'm quite sure. But wouldn't the lapis be prettier set in gold?"

Caitlin's head jerked up. "In gold, it will cost more than twice the amount."

"Let's look at some designs now. My mother likes her jewelry simple and delicate, rather than heavy and ornate. Whimsical, if you know what I mean."

Caitlin thought for a moment. "Does she have a pet?"

"A large red cat named Charlie. Does she ever dote on that beastie!"

"How about this?" Caitlin picked up her pencil, and with a few deft strokes brought to life a sleeping cat encircling a stone pillow.

His laughter boomed out, surprising her. "Aye, she'd like that."

"Do you think she'd prefer it as a brooch, or as a pendant on a chain?"

"A brooch, I think. So when can ye have it for me?"

Caitlin thought about the deadline for the Marcus-Pfeiffer order. Oh, well, this little piece shouldn't take too long. "Next week? Wednesday?"

"Wednesday it is, Miss…" He looked at the business cards on the table, "Miss Abernathy."

Caitlin became all business. "I'll need your name and address and a deposit."

"Dr. Stryker! What brings you to this part of town?" Aristotle stood in the doorway, filing it completely.

The man turned toward Aristotle with a laugh. "Good day to you, Aristotle. And I've told you before, the name's Colin. And I'm here orderin' a birthday present for my mother. Wasn't it you singin' the praises to me of Caitlin Abernathy and her designs?"

Aristotle saw Caitlin's look of confusion. "This is Dr. Stryker. I've told you about him. He's a visiting professor in history, here from St. Andrew's in Ireland for the year."

Caitlin glared at the professor. "You might have told me you knew Aristotle."

The deep laughter rolled again. "And if I had, would it have got me a better price?"

Caitlin shook her head. "No. Business is business."

"Fine by me. I like a woman who can keep her mind on the business at hand, whatever that business may be." His lips twitched at the corners again as if he were laughing at her.

Caitlin took his proffered credit card. Why did everything he said seem suggestive? She shrugged off the illogical feeling and methodically clicked off in her mind the cost of the little piece she had designed only moments ago. She added fifty percent for her workmanship and presented the bill to him. She held her breath. It was going to be a very expensive piece.

Hardly glancing at the bill, he said, "Fine." He took the machine from her, approved the full amount rather than just the deposit, and entered his pin number.

Caitlin smiled. It was the quickest six hundred fifty dollars she'd ever made.

"Thank you." Dr. Stryker's nod included both Aristotle and Caitlin. "I'll be back to pick up my little gold and lapis cat on Wednesday a week then." At the door he hesitated, turning back to gaze once more at Caitlin.

She was placing the lapis pieces back in the drawer with care, one at a time so as not to chip them. Her fingers touched something…something wrong. She prodded among the lapis and pulled out…what was it?

"What on earth?" She took the offending object out and looked at it. It was a dragon. About two inches long. Caitlin held the piece up to see it better.

Colin Stryker strode back into the shop. "Take it into your workroom. Let's see it under the light."

Caitlin didn't even think of objecting to the command in his voice. She laid the small piece down on her worktable. The two men crowded in to look at it.

"May I pick it up?" The professor took the piece and turned it slowly under the bright light. The three of them examined it from all angles.

The head, tail and crest of the dragon were all made of finely crafted gold, workmanship of a quality Caitlin had rarely seen in her life. On each point of the dragon's crest was a perfect, round, blood-red stone, five of them in all. Pigeon's blood rubies. They were very rare. She'd only read about them before, never seen one. But the body was the most amazing part. It was made of a single large baroque pearl. It could not be anything but authentic.

"This is a serious piece of jewelry," Caitlin said. "The gold and the rubies, they look too real to be anything but genuine. And the pearl is gorgeous. The workmanship on the gold is fantastic. But how did it get into my drawer, there among my lapis?"

"It's real, all right." Colin Stryker picked up Caitlin's magnifying glass and studied the designs worked into the gold. "It's real and it's very old. I think we may have an important piece of history here, but I can't be sure until I do some research. May I take it with me?"

Caitlin hesitated. "I'm not sure I want to give it up without knowing more about it. It must have been put in my drawer for a reason. Someone wanted me to have it."

"Possibly." Colin paused. "But you won't know where it came from until someone does some research on the piece. I know how to do that."

Still, Caitlin hesitated.

Colin sighed. "I'm a stranger to you and you don't trust me. Fair enough. Suppose we photograph the brooch and I give you a note as to where and when it was found, stating I have taken it for research purposes and will return it to you at a given time. The presumption is, it is yours, unless we find significant information to the contrary, possession being nine tenths the law and all that—"

Aristotle added, "You can trust Dr. Stryker, Caitlin. I'll get my camera and prepare an agreement."

Caitlin thought for a moment. Did she really want anything this valuable on the premises? Besides, if Aristotle thought Colin Stryker was all right, it was good enough for her.

"Agreed. Take it." Caitlin frowned. "But I just don't understand what it is doing in my shop. How did it get here?"

"Maybe if we find out what it is, we'll be able to deduce how it got here," the professor said with academic logic.

Aristotle took photographs of the piece from several angles and typed an agreement for Colin Stryker to sign. Caitlin wrapped the dragon in a piece of soft jeweler's felt and Colin slipped it into one of his shapeless jacket pockets.

"I'll call you when I know something." With that, he left.

****

Colin Stryker walked down College Avenue to where he'd parked his car, his mind in turmoil.

Caitlin. His heart had literally skipped a beat when he saw her. Her cloud of dark hair and those incredible amber eyes. And when she spoke, her voice, her soft, melodious voice...

Mother of God, what was he thinking? He was far too old for her. She couldn't be more than twenty-something and he was pushing forty. He was known to all his colleagues as a confirmed bachelor, and, until an hour ago, he'd have sworn he was happy to be so. He did not want the complication of a woman in his life.

Never again did he want the pain and devastation caused when Elizabeth had left him for another man. Years of numbness had followed. He'd welcomed that numbness; it allowed him to go on living. That and his work had saved him. He'd reached the stage where it no longer hurt, where it no longer mattered. After that, he'd thought he was impervious to women.

But Caitlin Abernathy...He was going to have to be very, very careful around Caitlin Abernathy.

Chapter Three

The next week was a busy one. Caitlin worked non-stop on the pieces for Marcus-Pfeiffer while Aristotle managed the shop. Evenings she worked on the little piece she had agreed to make for Dr. Stryker. He was an unusual man. She couldn't seem to get him out of her mind. He was reserved and formal in his manner, and yet, just below the surface, she sensed something very different. There was laughter and a passion for living he was for some reason holding sharply in rein.

She held up the piece of lapis, now polished to a rich sheen. The little gold cat lay sleeping soundly on it, falling slightly off the edge of the stone in the way cats do when they sleep, its tail curled around its legs. She was pleased with the effect and hoped Dr. Stryker would like it. And, more to the point, his mother would like it. He was to pick it up at five. She glanced at her watch. Good Lord. She'd had no idea it was so late. He'd be here any minute.

As if in answer to her thoughts, she heard the shop door open and Aristotle's voice. "Dr.Stryker! I think Caitlin's just about finished your piece. I'll go get her."

Caitlin took one more look at the little brooch and with a deep breath walked through to the shop.

"Good afternoon, Dr. Stryker. I've just finished your cat." She carefully set the piece of jewelry on a small velvet square.

"And a good day to you, Caitlin." His gaze lingered on her face for a moment. Then he seemed to recall what he was there for. He took the little piece in his hand and turned it this way and that.

"There is no upside or downside. You can turn it any way and it still looks right." He chuckled. "My mother will love this."

"If you look at the back, I've made the clasp so the brooch can be worn in any way she chooses. I've put on a safety clasp, of course, so it won't easily get lost. And here, see? I've put a small loop where your mother can run a chain through if she decides she'd like to wear it as a pendant."

"That's very thoughtful of you. Thank you."

"Is your mother here in Berkeley with you?"

"No. She's in Ireland. I'll have to send it to her. But she'll get it in good time."

"I'll gift wrap it. And put my card in it if you don't mind, so she'll know it was custom made."

Caitlin took the piece back into her workroom to gift wrap. So he was from Ireland. That explained the accent. She could hear Aristotle and the professor in muted conversation. She nestled the little cat in a box with her name on it, "Jewels by Caitlin," and wrapped it in lavender and rose tissue. She finished it with gold ribbon and held it up to examine. It would do.

Once they figured out what to do about the dragon, she likely wouldn't see him again. Just as well. After the experience with Allen, she didn't need another man in her life any time soon. Especially one as overpowering as Professor Stryker.

She walked back into the showroom with the little

box in her hand. "Here you are."

"Aye. Very pretty. Thank you."

"Have you had any luck finding anything about my dragon?"

"Yes, as a matter of fact, I have. I'm waiting for one last piece of evidence. I'll let you know as soon as I'm sure." He turned to leave.

At the door he hesitated, and turned back. "Why don't you both join me for dinner? It must be almost closin' time, and I do hate eatin' alone."

Aristotle shook his head. "I wish I could, Professor, but I've got a paper to finish."

"Too bad." The professor turned to Caitlin. "But perhaps you'd be free to join me?"

Caitlin hesitated for only a moment. She'd missed both lunch and breakfast. She was hungry.

****

Colin silently congratulated himself. She was having dinner with him. It was a first step.

A half hour later, settled at a table in Dundle's, Colin with a glass of ale in front of him, and Caitlin with a glass of red wine, they both ordered the special cheeseburger and fries with everything.

When the waitress left, Colin took a deep breath said, "So, Miss Abernathy…"

"Please. Call me Caitlin."

"So, Caitlin, if you don't mind my askin', how do you come to know Aristotle Jones?"

"Sheer good luck on my part. I needed somebody I could trust to work in the shop and live on the premises, to be a sort of guard at night, and Aristotle needed a job and a place to live so he could continue his graduate studies. I knew the minute he walked in he was the right one for the job. I mean, who wouldn't be intimidated by someone his size?"

Colin made a non-comital "Humph."

"Of course he's gentle as a lamb," Caitlin continued, "in addition to being one of the brightest men I've ever known, but that's not what anyone would think on first seeing him, is it? Those football-player shoulders and all those muscles? And dreadlocks? He told me he was down to his last cent and contemplating having to withdraw from university when he saw the 'Help Wanted' sign on my shop window. He's been with me for five years. I couldn't manage without him."

"So you're living together, are you?" He could have bit his tongue for the question, but too late. It was out. He had no right to be asking personal questions of this young woman. Was he out of his mind? He took a sip of his ale to cover his confusion.

Caitlin appeared unaware of his discomfort. She answered without hesitation. "No."

He couldn't suppress his sigh of relief. Thank goodness she hadn't taken offense at his very personal question.

She continued, "I live in a house left to me by my parents. It's in the Berkeley hills."

"Just clearin' the air. I wouldn't want to be steppin' on the toes of anyone the size of Aristotle." Colin couldn't believe what was coming out of his mouth. He had lost control over his tongue.

But Caitlin laughed. "Aristotle's a dear friend. But there's never been anything romantic between us. I'm not sure why. He's a wonderful man, but we've always, right from the beginning, been just friends. He sort of looks after me like a guardian angel."

He almost choked on his ale. "Sorry. The image of Aristotle wearin' white feathery wings was too much for me."

"So," Caitlin swallowed her mirth, "Do I call you Professor Stryker or Dr. Stryker or what?"

"Well, we could do it up right, like the Germans, '*Herr Professor Doctor*' Mr. Professor Doctor Stryker. But wouldn't it be easier just to call me Colin?"

"That's a relief. Colin it is."

"So I take it there's no boyfriend on the scene, then? Just to be clear on the subject."

Caitlin was silent.

Colin could have bit his tongue. "I'm sorry. I didn't mean to trespass." He had no right to ask such questions. It wasn't as if he…

"There was someone," Caitlin's subdued voice interrupted his thoughts. "He was murdered…I buried him just a week ago—" Her eyes filled with unshed tears.

"What…?"

She bit her lip and her features twisted as the story tumbled out, her horror and shock at the way Allen died visible on her features.

Colin listened, shocked, without interrupting. When she had finally wound down, he said, "I'm so sorry. I know what it is to lose someone you love."

Through her tears Caitlin said, "No. That's not it. You see the problem isn't I loved him and lost him. The problem is I didn't love him. I liked Allen. He was fun to be with, I relied on him more than I should have, but I didn't love him. Perhaps if I had been honest about my feelings, he might have found someone who could have loved him the way he deserved."

The silence lengthened. When Colin spoke, his voice was soft and unutterably sad. "We can't control who we love. Love's the most irrational of emotions. He chose to be with you. We each make our own choices. You have nothing to feel guilty about."

Colin cursed at himself inside. Bloody hell. How could he have been so insensitive with his crass questions? It would serve him right if she refused ever to see him again. And in spite of his determination not to come under the spell of any woman, he did very much want to see Caitlin Abernathy again.

They finished their meal in silence.

Colin paid the bill. It was his invitation, he insisted.

"I'm sorry to have dumped my problems on you. Thank you for listening." Caitlin sighed. "I have to get back to the shop. I have a little more work to do before I can call it finished for the night."

"I'll walk along with you. My car's parked near the shop."

****

The two of them strolled in amicable silence down College Avenue. As they approached the shop, the clanging of a burglar alarm made Caitlin's heart jump into her throat.

"What...?" Caitlin ran, Colin following close behind. The door to the shop was hanging crazily off its hinges.

Caitlin stood just inside the door, gulping for breath, surveying the damage. Her glass display cases had been smashed, their contents scattered. She navigated her way through the broken glass to her workroom and screamed, frozen to the spot.

Aristotle sat slumped, gagged and duct taped to a

33

chair, blood seeping through his thick hair. Then he looked up at her, eyes wide and frantic.

Colin pushed by her and yanked the gag off. Aristotle gasped for air.

"Scissors," Colin snapped.

Caitlin pulled herself out of her paralysis and reached in a drawer. Colin cut the tape binding Aristotle to the chair, and turned back to Caitlin. "Can't you turn off that damned clamorin'?"

Caitlin moved to the box on the wall and disabled the alarm. The silence was almost more shocking than the noise had been.

Aristotle half stood, but fell back into the chair. "Sorry. Dizzy."

"You're bleeding." Trying not to panic, Caitlin went into the bathroom and wet a cloth. Gently she pressed it to Aristotle's head, blotting the blood away. It was difficult to know how serious the wound was under all his hair, but the bleeding seemed to have stopped. "We need to call an ambulance. You need medical attention."

"No. No hospital. They'd shave my head where the wound is. No way. Just dump some alcohol on it."

Caitlin was already reaching into the drawer under the sink where she kept her first aid supplies. She pulled out a large alcohol swab, tore open its foil envelope and pressed it to the spot where Aristotle's hair was matted with blood.

Aristotle yelped. "Ouch! That stings!"

"It's meant to." Somehow, the simple act of attending to Aristotle's wound helped. "How does it feel?"

"It'll be fine. The knock on the head isn't what got

me. It just slowed me down. They injected me with something. I wasn't expecting that. Sorry, Caitlin. They made a real mess here."

For the first time Caitlin took a good look around her workroom. The cabinets had all been overturned, their drawers removed. Her stones lay everywhere, a jumble of color and light. A lot of good the alarm had done.

She swayed, light headed. Colin caught her, helped her to a chair and pushed her head down. "Breathe!"

The dizziness lessened and she looked up to two faces, one very brown, one very white, hovering over her.

Colin ineffectually patted her hand.

Aristotle put a damp cold cloth on her head. "It's not as bad as it looks, Caitlin. There's not much missing. Maybe nothing. We won't know for sure until we check the stones against the inventory list but I don't think robbery was involved. We'll have to replace the glass showcases, but I can fix the storage cabinets. And I'll fix the front door first thing."

Colin added, "I've called the police. They should be here shortly." He turned to Aristotle. "Do you know how many of them there were?

Aristotle grunted. "Just two. I think they may have been the same ones who attacked you, Caitlin. They'd never have taken me if they hadn't drugged me. I'm so sorry."

"It's not your fault, Aristotle. Who could have anticipated something like this?"

Colin stared at the chaos around him. "We need to think about this before the police arrive. If nothing was stolen, either this was a random act of vandalism, or the intruders were looking for something specific and didn't find it."

Caitlin shook the confusion out of her head. "What do you mean?"

"The dragon." Colin said. "Someone put it in among your semi-precious stones. Someone hid it there. And now, maybe, that same someone wants it back."

"Or maybe someone else wants it," Aristotle added. "After all, the person who put it there wouldn't have to trash the shop. He'd know right where it was. But others may have had only a general idea. They would have had to look everywhere. I came to as they were leaving. They were speaking in a sort of gutter French. I heard one of them say, *Merde. C'est pas ici!*"

"*Shit, it isn't here.* It's pretty obvious what they were looking for," Colin said.

"They were looking for the dragon?" Caitlin shook her head. "You both think this is about the dragon?"

"Almost certainly." Colin nodded. "And I think until we know more about it, we shouldn't mention the dragon to the police."

"You mean we should lie? To the police?"

"We don't have to lie, Caitlin. Nothing was stolen. As far as we can tell at this point, nothing is missing." Aristotle shrugged his shoulders. "Why confuse the issue?"

****

Two uniformed officers stepped gingerly through the broken door. "You the people who called? Officer Mulroney and Officer Brown." The officer who spoke indicated her younger, male partner. "You had some trouble here, I see."

"We were just out for a couple of hours for dinner." Caitlin shook her head in disbelief. "And when we came back..."

"Let's start at the beginning," the woman said. "You are?"

"I'm Caitlin Abernathy. This is my shop, and these two men are my assistant, Aristotle Jones, and a friend of ours, Dr. Colin Stryker."

A half hour later the police left, saying since nothing appeared to have been taken it could be assumed to have been a random act of vandalism. They would look into it, but finding the perpetrators was unlikely. They professed some surprise at this kind of crime in a neighborhood where theft and destruction of property were rare.

When the police left, the three of them sat down amidst the mess.

"What now?" Caitlin said.

"I'm not letting you go home alone," Aristotle said. "You go upstairs to bed. I changed my sheets just this morning. The place is reasonably tidy. You get some sleep."

In spite of herself, Caitlin yawned. "And where will you sleep?"

"I'm not sleepy. I'm going to stay down here and clean up this mess."

"And I'm going to help you," Colin added.

Chapter Four

The next morning when Caitlin awoke, she was at first disoriented by her surroundings, then shocked to see it was almost ten o'clock. Hastily she took off Aristotle's pajama top and put on the clothes she had been wearing yesterday. She'd go home to shower and change.

She descended the stairs to the shop. To her amazement, there was almost no evidence of the violence of the night before. The front door was, if not fully repaired, at least back on its hinges. Her showroom was devoid of its glass cases but was neat and tidy. She walked through to her workroom. The cabinets were once again upright, against the walls, and there were no loose stones in sight. The two men had worked a small miracle overnight.

Aristotle walked in, holding a bag from Starbucks. "Thought you might appreciate some coffee." He went through to the workshop and deposited two steaming cups and a pair of cinnamon twists on the table.

"Thank you, Aristotle. You're a lifesaver in more ways than one."

"No problem."

They pulled up two stools and munched on their morning repast.

Caitlin took a bite of her cinnamon twist and then a careful sip of her very hot coffee. "How's your head this morning? And how did you ever get the place back to this kind of order in just one night?"

"My head's just fine. And as to the shop, the professor helped. He didn't leave until after five this morning, and only then because he had an appointment with the Provost at nine."

Aristotle bit the end off his cinnamon twist and washed it down with a slug of coffee. "I've ordered a new showcase. Only one. Until we know what the insurance will cover, I thought we'd better be careful what we spend. Oh, and I've called the insurance company. They're sending an adjuster over this afternoon at four. You'd better be here. They probably won't want to deal with me about it. I have a copy of the police report, and the professor was sharp enough to take pictures of everything before we began cleaning up."

Caitlin sighed. "I don't remember what I'm paying you, Aristotle, but it's not nearly enough."

He laughed. "No problem, Caitlin, but a small raise would be much appreciated once your Marcus-Pfeiffer thing pays off."

"You've got a deal. Now I'd better go home to change if I'm to be back here at four. You'll be here to help me with the insurance people?"

"Of course, if you want me to be. Meanwhile I'll catch a little shut-eye. It's been a long night. We'll put the 'Closed' sign on the door."

****

Back in her house in the Berkeley hills, Caitlin took a long hot shower and changed into worn jeans and a sweater. Maybe, instead of returning to the shop right away, she could work at home on designs for the

Marcus & Pfeiffer Christmas Catalogue collection. She walked through the living room to her workroom, and perched on the high bench at her worktable. She looked absently at the blank paper, her mind filled not with designs but with the chaos of the last twenty-four hours. Sighing, she lifted her eyes to the wide window, and gazed down the hills to the distant busy waters of the San Francisco Bay. She never tired of the view.

She loved this brown-shingled house with its surrounding, overgrown flowerbeds and tall fragrant eucalyptus trees. If she closed her eyes she could almost smell her mother's cookies and feel her warm hugs. And how patient her father had been as he sat beside her, his arm loosely around her shoulder, helping her with her hated math homework. "Just try it again," he'd say, pointing to a figure on the page. "Here's where you went wrong."

During her teen years, her cozy, safe world fell apart. First she became aware of stony silences between her parents. They had never been openly affectionate, but now they never touched and they spoke to each other only when necessary. Then came the loud arguments, cut off abruptly when they realized she could hear them. She knew something was seriously wrong between them. Still, she'd been shocked when they told her they planned to separate. Her father wanted a divorce. It seemed there was someone else—

The divorce never happened. Instead, they had died together in a horrific automobile accident on a foggy night on Highway 101. Ten years ago this month. She'd been just eighteen. She'd had to grow up fast.

Her parents left the house to her. She'd taken this little room, which used to be her father's office, as her workspace. She'd changed it in no way except to place her high drafting table and bench where her father's desk had once been, facing the view.

Sometimes, being so alone in the world, with no family or close friends, got to her in a visceral way. She had no one but Aristotle. She'd had no time for friends when she was in university. Every moment she hadn't been doing course work, she had been working on mastering the techniques of jewelry design and creation. Maybe that's why she'd drifted so willingly into a relationship with Allen. And now he was gone too. Caitlin wiped her eyes and blew her nose.

She brought her mind forcibly back to the task at hand. *Stop feeling sorry for yourself! You have work to do.*

Soon her pencil was flying. She sketched a possibility, then add notes as to which stones she would use, whether the medium would be gold, silver or copper, whether it was to be a pin, a necklace, a pendant, or earrings. Or whether it might be a matched set. She tended to avoid matched sets. When she did one, it was never more than two pieces. Earrings and a necklace, or necklace and bracelet, but never all three of the same design. That was just overkill. It tended to make the pieces look gaudy, no matter how fine the workmanship. As she thought, her hand moved over the pages. Some of these hasty drawings she'd discard, others she'd draw later in greater detail. Now she was just getting rough ideas down on paper.

She thought about the little cat piece she had made for Colin Stryker. Perhaps she should do a series of cat pieces. Cats could twist themselves into the most remarkable positions. They were natural models. And cat lovers bought cat jewelry. She smiled as her ideas tumbled out onto the paper.

Her stomach growled. What time was it? Three thirty! Where had the day gone? She had to get back to the shop, and she'd still had nothing to eat today except a cinnamon twist.

Her phone rang. "Caitlin Abernathy."

"Oh good, I caught you." It was Colin's deep, unmistakable voice.

"I was just about to leave for the shop. I'm meeting with the insurance adjusters at four."

"Good. I'll pick you up at five and we'll have dinner. I've made some interesting discoveries about our small friend."

"Our small…? Oh, yes, of course. Dinner would be wonderful. I'm starving." Caitlin glanced down at her jeans and scuffed running shoes and ran upstairs to change. Ten minutes later she looked into her full-length mirror. The clinging burgundy knit dress did wonders for her figure. She decided to leave her shoulder-length hair down.

Whether it was due to Caitlin's charm or Aristotle's intimidating presence, the insurance adjustor gave them little trouble. After her five hundred dollar deductible, the insurance company agreed to cover the replacement costs for her three showcases and a new shop door.

"Weren't we all fortunate none of your large investment in semi-precious stones went missing?" the adjustor said.

Caitlin was seeing the obsequious little man with his balding head and his smarmy manner out the door as Colin arrived.

"I have quite a bit to share with you both," Colin said, "but let's do it over dinner. I'm starved. I hope you can join us, Aristotle. I think you should hear this."

"Sure. I turned my paper in today, so I've got some breathing space. And I'm hungry, too."

"Up for Mexican?" Caitlin took her jacket off the coat rack in the workroom. Most restaurants were overly air-conditioned. "There's a place down on the marina…"

****

A half hour later, Caitlin and Colin were nursing margaritas while Aristotle sipped orange juice. All three dipped chips into salsa as they waited for their main courses to arrive.

"I've had a busy week and I've made some rather interesting discoveries." Colin paused and gave what Caitlin could only think of as a Cheshire-cat smile.

"So?" she said.

"Your little dragon once very likely belonged to Marie Antoinette." He sat back, waiting for shock and surprise.

Caitlin obliged. "You mean 'Let them eat cake' Marie Antoinette, the French Queen?"

Aristotle shook his head. "She never said that, Caitlin. It was just one of many lies the revolutionaries spread to make her look heartless. Marie Antoinette was an intelligent woman, far brighter than her doddering husband."

"Right on all scores," Colin said. "In 1792, a mob stormed the French Royal Treasury and stole the crown and the scepter, along with a number of other pieces. Your little piece wasn't among those, however. Most of those pieces were later sold into private hands by the

43

French government as insurance against the restoration of the monarchy. Crazy when you think about it. They went on later to accept an emperor and a new monarchy before they ever got their act together as a republic."

Their food arrived and they all took a moment to relish the aromas of enchiladas and chiles rellenos and refried beans.

Caitlin ladled sour cream and salsa liberally onto her food. "So if it wasn't among the pieces stolen, where did it come from? What makes you think Marie Antoinette had anything to do with it?"

"How much do you know about French history, Caitlin?"

"Not much."

"I know quite a lot," Aristotle volunteered, "but don't let that stop you, Colin."

"Well, to give you a very abbreviated version"— Colin took a deep breath and plunged in—"on October fifth, seventeen ninety-one, a rabble descended on the Palace at Versailles, where the royal family, King Louis, his queen, Marie Antoinette, their two children and their all courtiers were in residence. At that time, quite a bit of the queen's personal jewelry simply disappeared. The Royal Family was removed forcibly to Paris, where they took up residence in the Tuileries Palace. They were comfortably enough housed there, with a reduced court, but they were essentially living under house arrest." Colin took a large forkful of his enchilada and savored it.

"So that's when my little dragon was stolen from Versailles?"

"Probably not."

"Well, get on with it!" Caitlin plunked her glass

down on the table.

Aristotle grinned. "Patience was never Caitlin's long suit. If you have a point, you'd better get to it."

Colin gave her a wary glance. "You have to remember, Caitlin, I'm an historian. We're a long-winded lot. We don't know how to 'get on with it'." He took a sip of his margarita. "Anyway, numerous people worried about the safety of the king and queen and their family. Several escape plans were put forward, but the king was slow to act, and when he finally agreed, he insisted they travel as befitted their station, with everything but the proverbial kitchen sink. It was in June, 1791. They were caught less than ten miles from what is now the German border. If they'd traveled lighter, less ostentatiously, the whole of European history would probably have played out differently…"

"To hell with the whole of European history, Colin. My dragon, what about my dragon?"

"Ah yes, your dragon. By the way, what makes you think it's *your* dragon?

"Maybe the fact that I found it in one of *my* drawers? You claim to know history. You must be aware throughout history ownership has often hinged on little more than possession. Just think about the British Museum and the Elgin Marbles stolen from the Greeks, and the Russian collection of Impressionists 'liberated' from the Nazis at the end of WWII and never returned to the Jewish families who were their rightful owners."

"You have a point. For the moment at least, it is your dragon, although, strictly speaking, by your reasoning it is now *my* dragon, since it is in my possession."

"No. I have a receipt from you stating clearly, I have put my dragon in your hands solely for purposes of research."

"Hmm. So you did." He looked at her warily and cleared his throat. "To get back to the king and queen—"

"Must we?"

"I'm afraid we must if you're to understand what I'm going to propose."

"You're going to propose? Oh, Colin, this is so sudden!"

Aristotle glowered at her. "Behave yourself, Caitlin." To the professor he said, "I should have warned you what she's like after one margarita. She doesn't hold her alcohol well."

Again Caitlin watched the corners of Colin's mouth twitch. What did he find so damned amusing about her? "Well, get on with it," she snapped.

"Yes. Well, their attempted flight gave the radicals all the evidence they needed to stir things up. They broke into the Tuileries Palace on August tenth, 1792, forcing the royal family to take refuge in the Legislative Assembly. The revolutionaries murdered the Swiss Guards who had been charged with keeping the royals safe."

"So my dragon was stolen then?"

"Patience, patience. Under the guise of acting to protect them, the government moved the royal family to the tower of the Temple in the Marais. This was no palace. It was a jail. They had almost no attendants left to them this time. They were forced to live under simple, even harsh, conditions. One woman was allowed access, the wife of the British Ambassador,

Lady Elizabeth Leveson-Gower. Lady Elizabeth brought linen and clothes for the royal family, who were reduced to begging. Now it becomes interesting…"

"About time," Caitlin muttered.

Colin ignored her. "The story has it Marie Antoinette somehow managed to hide a few of her jewels on her person during the last, frantic move. She gave these to Lady Elizabeth, two bags, one of pearls and one of diamonds, to take back to England to keep safe for her. The Ambassador's wife would not be subject to a customs search by the Republican Militia because she had diplomatic immunity. I believe your dragon may have been among those pearl pieces."

Aristotle interrupted. "Why send them to England?"

"I expect she hoped to find refuge in England. It hadn't yet occurred to her their very lives were in danger."

He took a sip of his margarita, and continued. "Of course, Marie Antoinette never lived to reclaim her jewels. Her husband was guillotined on January twenty-eighth, 1793. Marie Antoinette was transferred to a cell in the Conciergerie, and she followed her husband to the guillotine a few months later."

Caitlin was silent for a moment. Somehow she had never before thought of Marie Antoinette as a real person. "What became of her children?"

"The little prince, who would have been King Louis XVII, died in prison two years later of neglect and maltreatment. The princess was sent back to Austria, where her mother came from. Exiled from France, she married and she lived to the ripe the old age

47

of 72, always hoping for the restoration of the monarchy."

"And the dragon?" Aristotle brought them back to the subject.

"Ah, yes, the amulet. It didn't bring much luck to the queen, did it?" Colin gave a mirthless smile.

Caitlin almost jumped out of her chair. "The *what*? What did you call it?"

"Why, the amulet. The dragon. It was supposed to have been a good luck charm."

"Amulet!" Caitlin shouted. "Amulet, Aristotle. That's what Allen said. *Amulet*, not omelet."

Colin looked from one to the other of them. "Would you mind telling me what you're talking about?"

"When Allen was"—Caitlin stumbled over the word—"murdered—"

"Yes?" Colin was clearly puzzled.

Aristotle interjected, "The police reported his last words were, 'must warn Caitlin...the omelet.' Don't you see? He didn't say *omelet*, he said *amulet*."

"Good grief! You think your boyfriend hid the dragon in among your stones?"

"It looks that way," Caitlin admitted reluctantly.

"Maybe I'd better tell you the rest of the history of this little amulet. It may have some bearing on what we do next."

"Please." Caitlin was suddenly very sober. "Tell us what happened. The Queen gave it to a friend. Then what?"

"Well, Lady Elizabeth's descendants held the jewels for several generations, but eventually released some for sale. In 1938, the dragon was sold in an auction at Sotheby's to American industrialist, Kenneth Newton. By the way, it sold for eight hundred thousand dollars. In today's money that would be several millions." Colin fumbled around in his briefcase. "Here. I found a photograph of it on line from the Sotheby's catalogue for the auction." Colin passed the photo to Caitlin.

"That's it. That's my dragon." She passed the photocopy on to Aristotle, who glanced at it and waited for the professor to continue.

"Newton died in a boating accident in 1964. The dragon was sold by his family, in a private sale for an undisclosed amount to the Countess Gabrielle Jouet, Chateau Beausejour, in the Loire Valley. She was murdered in her bed in 1977. A crime never solved. In her will, she left the amulet to the Louvre. And that's where it belongs. It's a piece of French history."

"It doesn't seem to have brought much luck to anyone who's owned it," Caitlin commented.

"No, it hasn't. It's said to have a curse on it."

"That's absurd," Caitlin countered.

"Don't be too quick to dismiss curses, Caitlin."

Caitlin chose to ignore his silly comment about curses. "None of its history tells us how it got from the Louvre to me. Or how Allen came to have it. Or why he put it in my drawer full of lapis. It just doesn't make any sense."

Colin took a deep breath and said, "There's more to the story. Six years ago, it was stolen from the Louvre in an aborted heist. Three men were involved. Two were caught on the scene with a number of priceless jewels in their possession—Napoleon's and Josephine's crowns, the Regent Diamond, and assorted other royal pieces. But one man got away. He had Marie Antoinette's little dragon with him."

He paused and considered Caitlin. "Could the third man have been your Allen? It all fits."

"Allen? Don't be absurd. He was an accountant."

"How do you know he was an accountant? Did you ever visit his office? Did he ever do any accounting for you? What do you know of his background, his family? Where did he come from?"

Caitlin shook her head. She looked down at the remaining untouched food on her plate. Her stomach was in turmoil and, once again the tears, so near the surface since Allen's death, threatened. She'd known Allen for four months, and she knew nothing about him. She'd accepted what he told her. He worked for a large accounting firm. He'd always been vague about the details. Their conversations were about everyday things. When she asked about his past, his family, he somehow always managed to divert the conversation. The vastness of her ignorance about him hit her. And yet he had cared for her. Of that one fact she was certain. The tears spilled over.

Aristotle pulled her to him as if she were a child, and comforted her. Looking over her head buried against his ample chest, he said to Colin, "Caitlin is the trusting kind. She's never quite realized not everything is as it seems. It's one reason I keep a close eye on her."

Colin sighed. "It's not a character flaw, trustin' in people." He signaled for the bill and paid it before Aristotle could remonstrate.

"Thank you for dinner." Aristotle wrapped Caitlin's sweater around her shoulders. "I think we should leave Caitlin's car at the shop and take her home, if you don't mind. I don't want her driving. She's had more to drink than usual and she's distraught."

"Of course. It's no problem at all. You do feel responsible for her, don't you?"

"She's got no one else."

"I have family all through Ireland and Brittany, scattered, but always there for me. I can't imagine how hard it must be to be so alone." Colin drove in silence through Berkeley and up into the hills, Aristotle giving terse directions as needed.

****

Caitlin nodded off during the drive and woke with a start. "Oh. We're here."

She pushed the car door open before Colin could get around the car to open it for her. Colin and Aristotle joined her on the sidewalk.

"Don't bother," she said. "I can let myself in,"

"I thought I'd stay the night," Aristotle answered. "I can sleep on that old sofa in the living room."

"I don't need a nursemaid, Aristotle."

"No." Colin's voice was firm. "But a couple of body guards might not be amiss in view of what's happened. I'm stayin' too."

Caitlin had her keys in her hand. "You're both being ridiculous."

The front door swung open to her touch without her unlocking it.

Aristotle pushed Caitlin into Colin's arms. "Stay put, you two. I'm going to look around."

Colin tightened his arms around Caitlin. He watched over her shoulder through the open door as Aristotle moved stealthily into the hall, and then on silent feet toward the living room.

Aristotle flicked the light switch. "No! Not again!"

"What's wrong?" Caitlin's voice was muffled against Colin's rough tweed jacket. He smelled so…male. His arms encircling her were strong and warm and comforting, but not very brotherly. Not like Aristotle's. His grasp tightened and a small shuddering sigh escaped his lips.

Aristotle was back at the front door. "Okay. Nobody's here. You can come in. But Caitlin, they've trashed your place. I'm sorry."

"No. Goddammit! No!" She ran in to the living room. Bookcases upended, books scattered all over the floor. Sofa cushions slashed. Pictures off the wall, their back panels pulled off. Tables overturned. Even the oriental carpet was bunched up. Clearly they had searched under it.

Caitlin hurried through to her office. She gave a sigh of relief when she saw her designs, her drawings were untouched. But here as in the living room, the books were all over the floor.

The kitchen was a disaster area. She stood in the doorway, speechless at the destruction. Shards of dishes and glassware made walking a challenge. Her flour and sugar canisters were upended, creating a fine film of dust over everything. Cabinets were swept clean, bran flakes and rice and cans of tomatoes and beans strewn haphazardly about. The fridge and freezer doors hung crazily open, their contents spilled out with the rest of the mess on the ceramic tile floor.

Turning her back on the chaos of the kitchen, she sprinted upstairs, followed closely by Colin and Aristotle. She stopped in disbelief at her bedroom door.

Her clothes had been flung in a haphazard heap on the floor, the dresses ripped off their hangers, pockets of all her pants turned inside out. Drawers were pulled out of her dresser, their contents adding to the jumble on the floor. Her jewelry lay in a tangle on her bed. At a quick glance nothing seemed to be missing, but the wanton damage was shocking. At least they hadn't slashed her bed or ripped her pillows apart. She sighed and walked through to her bathroom. Pills and capsules lay strewn about on her vanity, their empty bottles dropped on the counter or floor. God, what a mess! It would take weeks to sort it all out.

She turned to the other two bedrooms, Colin and Aristotle following on her heels. The beds were pulled apart but the mattresses and pillows were not slashed here either as the downstairs furniture was. The chests of drawers were untouched.

"I suppose I should be grateful they didn't wreck the guest bedrooms," she said.

"Looks like they were running out of time," Aristotle answered. "They didn't quite finish the job. I think they may have left by the back door when they heard our car pull up in front."

"All the more reason for Caitlin to have our protection here tonight." Colin righted an overturned chair. "It's going to be hard to explain this to the police."

Caitlin sighed. "And to the insurance company. I wonder what they'll say. It's too much of a coincidence."

"Maybe we should just clean it up and forget about reporting it." Aristotle looked around at the chaos the intruders had created. "You've been saying for months you wanted to get rid of those two chairs and that old beaten down sofa in the living room. Look on this as a golden opportunity to redecorate. The rest of the house just needs putting back together." He looked at Colin. "You game for another night's work?"

Colin laughed. "Sure, an' why not? I agree we should leave the insurance company and the police out of it."

It took four hours to restore some semblance of order to the downstairs. When the job was done, they sat in the minimally tidy kitchen sipping mugs of lemon ginger tea.

"I know our agreement was I'd return the dragon to you as soon as I'd completed my research," Colin said, "but it's hidden in a secure place at the university and I think we should leave it there for the time being. It's not safe to have it near you."

Caitlin looked at him. "You think that's what this is all about?"

"It's the only thing that makes sense. Why else would anyone be searching your home and your shop?"

"So whoever wants the dragon knows I have it?"

"At least they suspect you may have it. And because they do, I'm not going to leave you alone in this house," Colin announced. "I saw three bedrooms upstairs. I'm staying here until further notice. Just think of it as havin' a boarder."

Aristotle put his mug down on the table. "Good idea, Colin. One of us can be with her at all times. We'll both stay here tonight, but I'll go back to the shop tomorrow morning. That way she'll have one of us with her in the shop and one of us here. Between us we can keep her safe until this is resolved."

Caitlin banged her hands down on the table. "I don't think I can deal with the amount of testosterone flying about the kitchen at this moment. If you two *gentlemen* are through discussing who will take care of poor little me, talking about me as if I'm not even here, you can both just get out now. I'm perfectly capable of taking care of myself. I'm going to bed, and I'd better not see either of your ugly faces over my morning coffee. Good night, Aristotle. Good night, Colin. Go home. Both of you. I've had enough."

Caitlin stormed out of the room. She clumped up the stairs and slammed her bedroom door shut.

The two men sat in stunned silence for a moment. Then Aristotle spoke. "You take the back bedroom; I'll take the middle one."

"Right."

They washed their teacups and took off their shoes so Caitlin wouldn't hear them on the stairs.

****

The short, fat man ground out his cigarette in an already overflowing ashtray.

"*Rien*! Nothing. Nothing in her shop, nothing in her house, and now nothing here. Where the hell could he have hidden it?" He looked around the apartment in Oakland they had just tossed for the second time.

Jules glared at his accomplice. "You and your knife." His tone was waspish, accusatory. "If you'd let me work on him with the drug we might have found out whether he still had it and where it was, but no. You had to have your fun with him. By the time I got to question him he was already half dead."

"He gave us her name," his partner answered defensively. "How many Caitlins can there be around here? And her name and address were on his iPhone."

"The fact he kept saying her name as he was dying doesn't signify anything. He was likely just repeating his girlfriend's name. Look at this place. What do you see?"

Nic glanced around with distaste at their surroundings. "It's a dump. Even before we searched it, it was a dump."

"Exactly. If he had the dragon, would he be living like this? He'd sell the piece to a collector or he'd break it up and sell the jewels separately. He had the connections. He could have been living like a king. Living like this—it just doesn't make any sense."

"That's why it took us so long to locate him. He should have been living it up in some posh resort." The short man lit another cigarette and inhaled deeply, suppressing a cough. "Maybe he lost all his money gambling?"

"Alain? Never. He was not a gambling man. I'm beginning to suspect he never had the dragon. We know he got away when the *flics* ambushed us, but we don't know for a fact he had the missing piece with him. Anything could have happened to it. A crooked cop could have pocketed it. A museum employee. All we know is the newspapers said it was missing. They're the only ones who connected it to Alain."

They sat in silence for a few minutes.

Jules sighed. "Anyway, we did what we set out to do. We killed the *cochon*. We've paid him back for setting us up, for those five years we spent in prison."

"I just wish he admitted taking the dragon before he kicked off. I don't like loose ends. I say we write this off now. Let's go back to Paris. There's nothing more for us here." Jules stood and stretched.

"Maybe." Nic took a drag on his cigarette. "But there's something about that girl…my gut tells me she's hiding something. It might be nothing but maybe it's worth a few more days' surveillance, *non?*"

Chapter Five

The next morning Caitlin woke with a pounding headache. She refused to attribute it to the margaritas. It was a tension headache. She pawed through the bottles scattered on the counter, picked up a prescription bottle, and looked at the date. It had expired five years before. At least the mess would force her to get rid of stuff she should have tossed years ago. Then she saw the distinctive red cap. Tylenol. Thank God. She poured a glass of water and gulped down two pills.

By the time she had showered, washed her hair, and slipped into a loose blue sweater and jeans, she felt somewhat more human. She pulled her hair back into the ponytail she wore when she wasn't in her professional uniform. She was glad she had sent Aristotle and Colin home last night. They were being ridiculous. She could very well take care of herself, and she was looking forward to a quiet morning alone.

In the kitchen, she made a pot of coffee and put a slice of whole grain bread into the toaster. She was just taking the first bite of her toast when the doorbell rang.

"Miss Caitlin Abernathy?" It was the same two policemen she'd first spoken to. The ones who'd informed her of Allen's death.

"Detective O'Malley and Officer Thurgood, isn't it?" Caitlin said. "Please come in. Have a seat." She indicated a tattered sofa cushion on the floor as if its condition were of no consequence. "Pardon the state of the place, I'm redecorating."

"I think we'll remain standing, ma'am. What happened here?"

"It's pretty obvious, isn't it? Someone trashed my place last night."

"Isn't this the second B&E you've had recently? Seems to me I saw something about your shop being broken into. Is someone targeting you?"

"You tell me." Caitlin shrugged her shoulders. "So if you aren't here about the vandalism in my home and in my shop, what can I do for you?"

"It's about your former boyfriend," the older detective said.

Caitlin winced. Whether at the officer's tone or at the word *boyfriend*, she wasn't sure. She braced herself for whatever was coming. "You mean Allen Thompson?"

"Yes, the man you knew as Allen Thompson."

"What about him? I've already told you everything I know about him."

Colin sauntered downstairs at that moment. "Good morning, Caitlin. I see we have company."

"What are you doing here?" Caitlin hissed. "I thought I told you to go home last night."

"I just couldn't bear to leave you." He leaned over and gave her a smacking kiss on the cheek.

Caitlin opened her mouth to object, but wasn't quite sure what she was objecting to.

"Do I smell coffee?" Colin headed toward the kitchen. "Can I offer either of you officers a coffee?"

The older officer frowned. "You are?"

"We met when you came to question Ms.

Abernathy in her shop. I'm Colin Stryker, a friend of Miss Abernathy's."

"Oh, yes. The history professor. Well, Dr. Stryker, I just wondered if Miss Abernathy knew Allen Thompson by his other name."

"His other name?" In spite of her annoyance with Colin, Caitlin was suddenly alert. Waiting for the next blow.

Aristotle, who had come down the stairs so quietly no one had heard him, repeated her question. "What other name?"

The policeman jerked around to stare at the latest arrival on the scene. "You're the one who lives over the shop, aren't you? Jones. Something Jones."

"Aristotle Jones. Yes. I live over Miss Abernathy's shop. But I stayed here last night."

"Both of you stayed over last night?" Officer Thurgood's expression was somewhere between shock and envy.

Colin brought them back to the topic. "You said something about Allen Thompson?"

The detective answered. "His real name is Alain Tremont and the French police and Interpol have been looking for him for the last six years."

Caitlin took a shuddering breath. "The French police? But Allen told me he was Canadian. What did the French police want him for?"

"Alain Tremont was French and he had a record as long as your arm. He was a burglar who specialized in stealing jewelry from the unoccupied rooms of the rich and famous. A non-violent criminal. Somehow he got involved with two decidedly violent men who were planning a robbery at the Louvre in Paris six years ago.

How or why he teamed up with them, no one knows. Probably just couldn't resist the temptation of the Louvre collection."

"Allen?" Caitlin's voice shook. "Allen Thompson was a jewel thief?"

"The name's Tremont. Alain Tremont," Detective O'Malley corrected her. "To make a long story short, the Paris police got a tip and caught him in the bedroom of a well-known socialite, with his hands full of diamonds. To escape a long prison sentence he cut a deal with the police and agreed to help them catch his fellow thieves in the act."

Aristotle broke in, "So he did what the police asked?"

The officer gave a mirthless laugh. "Not quite. It was no part of the deal with the police he should get away scot free with a trinket worth several million dollars. As you can imagine, no one was happy about that, not the Louvre, not the Paris police, and certainly not his co-conspirators, who were pretty pissed off, if you'll pardon my French."

Caitlin sensed Colin and Aristotle closing in on her, standing on either side of her like sentinels. Aristotle put his arm around her shoulder, and Colin took her hand.

It was Colin who spoke. "I'm sure you can appreciate Miss Abernathy had a very difficult day yesterday, and now this shock. If you have nothing more—"

"Oh, but we do have more. We can deal with it here, or we can take her in. How would you have it?"

Caitlin shrugged Aristotle's arm away and pulled her hand from Colin's grasp. She stepped away from her two defenders, turning briefly to glare at each of them in turn.

She spoke directly to Detective O'Malley. "I'll assist in you any way I can. What do you want of me?"

"Just some help with a couple of pictures." O'Malley motioned to his fellow officer.

Officer Thurgood handed two photographs to Caitlin. "Do you know either of these men?"

Caitlin took only a moment. "They're the ones outside my shop. The ones who knocked me down and took my sample case."

Aristotle peered over her shoulders. "And that's who attacked me in the shop."

"Thank you," Detective O'Malley said. "This one"—he pointed to the photograph of the tall cadaverous man, the one who had pushed Caitlin down—"this one's Jules Allard. He's known to be extremely violent. This other one, the plump one with the jolly face, is Nic Bisset. I understand he's very good with a knife. Now, these two gentlemen spent five years in a French prison because of your boyfriend. You can see how they might be a trifle annoyed."

He dropped the sarcastic note from his voice. "We want those men for homicide and for arson. If you know anything, anything at all, that can lead us to them, tell us now."

Caitlin shook her head. "I didn't know about Allen, that is, Alain. I had no idea…"

The officer's eyes bored into her. "I didn't think you did, but I had to ask. Obviously, these two break-ins of yours are somehow related. Could you unknowingly be in possession of something those two want? Perhaps the little piece of jewelry Alain stole from the Louvre?"

Aristotle's hand tightened on Caitlin's shoulder and Colin reached again for her hand. Caitlin stood mute.

"Well, if you think of anything…"

Aristotle walked the two officers to the door. "Thank you."

O'Malley paused in the doorway. "It might be a good idea for the young lady to go stay with friends for a while. That French pair could well have it in for her if they got her name out of Tremont before killing him."

****

After the cops drove away, Aristotle and Colin looked at each other. Colin spoke. "We can't tell them about the amulet."

Caitlin turned to face them, hands on her hips. "What's this 'we' stuff? It's my place to tell them or not to tell them. It's my amulet. Would you two stop talking as if I'm not here?"

"But…" Colin said.

"Caitlin…" Aristotle said at the same time.

Colin repeated, "We can't tell them."

"In God's name, why not?" Caitlin shouted. "We all know now what they're searching for. Nothing else makes any sense. First my shop, then my home. Allen's last words were warning me about this. We need to tell them everything."

"And then?" Colin said.

"Well, then I suppose they'll want to take the amulet as evidence." Caitlin's voice slowed as she spoke.

Aristotle pushed on. "Do you know how many times objects held in evidence rooms by the police in the US have disappeared? If you think I'm being paranoid, just do a Google search. If the dragon falls into the hands of your average thief, it will be broken down and its jewels sold separately. Its historic value will be lost forever."

Colin picked up Aristotle's thought. "And even if the dragon were to be held safely, even if it didn't disappear while in custody, who would it be returned to when some trial at some distant unknown date was over?" Colin was pacing as he spoke. "It would probably end up in the Smithsonian, like most of the rest of Marie Antoinette's jewels, like the Hope Diamond, which I might add was another of the French royal jewels that disappeared during the bloodbath referred to as the French Revolution, only to resurface and remain in America."

"So what do you think we should do?" Caitlin was confused and exhausted. Her head was pounding and she just wanted to go to back to bed.

"We'll have to cooperate with the police. You need their protection. But we don't have to mention the dragon."

"But what should we do with it?" Caitlin looked from one man to the other. "As long as we have it, we're in danger. They said those two men—what were their names? Nic Bisset and Jules Allard—were seriously bad."

"I might point out neither you nor Aristotle has the dragon, Caitlin," Colin said in an infuriatingly reasonable tone. "I have it, and it's well hidden. And so far, I don't think the thieves even know of my existence. It's you they're after."

"Well, thanks. That's reassuring," Caitlin

answered, sarcasm dripping from her voice. "You've certainly made me feel a lot safer."

"Caitlin, we don't intend to let anything bad happen to you. Aristotle and I will keep watch over you night and day until this matter is resolved."

"My knights in shining armor." Caitlin meant to glower at them, but she giggled instead. Colin in his musty tweeds and Aristotle in his multicolored shirt and cords. A fine pair of knights they were. She smothered her laughter. "So what should we do with this good luck charm? It doesn't seem to have brought much luck to Marie Antoinette, or to Allen or to any of its previous owners." The memory of Allen and of what happened to him brought her back to reality of their situation.

Colin put his arm around her in a brief hug. "I know," he said. "It's all been horrible. That's because so far, they've been acting and we've been reacting. The time has come for us to act."

Aristotle nodded agreement.

"You two have cooked something up."

Aristotle smiled. "If you mean we've done some strategic planning, you're correct. The amulet was stolen from the Louvre. It should be returned to the Louvre."

Caitlin's mouth dropped open. She took a deep breath. "You mean we're just going to take it to France, bypassing the police and customs officers of two countries, not to mention some very bad characters dogging our trail, and waltz into the museum it was stolen from with the trinket in our hands? Sure. That sounds like a plan. Are you out of your blooming minds?"

Colin continued as if she hadn't spoken. "I know

the curator of the historic jewelry collection there. I can turn it over directly to her. She'll be only too happy to welcome it back. We'll get lots of newspaper coverage about its return."

"Once it's back where it belongs, and the thieves know it is there, you'll be safe. We're only targets now because they think we, that is"—Colin pointed a finger at Caitlin—"they think *you* have it. And why do they think you have it? Your Allen/Alain must have told them where he hid it. It's the only possible answer."

"Well, that makes me feel a lot safer. Thanks, guys."

"The detective suggested it might be a good idea for you to get out of the line of fire for a little while," Aristotle said, the voice of reason.

"He was suggesting I get out of my house, stay with friends, not take off on an international jaunt. In fact, I suspect the police might take a very dim view of my traveling internationally right now, with an unsolved murder in the picture."

"We just thought a little trip to Paris might be in order, a short trip," Colin said. "They won't even miss us before we're back."

"Are you both crazy? I have work to do. I have an order to fill for Marcus-Pfeiffer. I have commissions to complete. I'm a working girl, in case neither of you noticed. I can't just up and go to Paris. No. No way. Just forget about it."

Aristotle continued as if Caitlin hadn't spoken. "It shouldn't take you away from your work for more than a few days. You wouldn't even have to go with us except we don't want to leave you here unprotected."

"You're insane, both of you! You're stark raving

mad. I won't even discuss this with you any further."

"We understand," Colin soothed. "Why don't you go into your studio and work for a while? Get some of those designs done for the collection you're working on. We'll call you when breakfast is ready. You have eggs?"

"Of course I have eggs!" Caitlin found herself shouting. They were plotting something. She was sure of it. She shot a poisonous look from one to the other.

She stomped into her studio. They were infuriating. She perched on the stool at her drafting table and suddenly found laughter bubbling up. When and how had this absurd partnership come about? One of them could lie and the other would swear to it. Still, it was comforting having them underfoot.

They were so silly in their overprotectiveness. Two huge bumbling males. As if she couldn't look after herself! *Poor little me!* She'd never quite pictured herself as a damsel in distress. And even if she had, one hero would have sufficed. Not two. Certainly not these two. Neither one of them was any girl's vision of Prince Charming, the one in his rumpled tweeds, the other with his dreadlocks. They were being silly. But somehow she knew she would sleep better knowing they were near.

She doodled absently as her mind drifted to the beautiful little dragon who was at the heart of all this trouble. Perhaps she could do a series of little dragons. Tails switching, heads curled 'round. Some rampant and some sleeping. Her pencil flew over the paper. She couldn't use rubies and pearls but they'd be charming set with chalcedony and amethysts. Or perhaps moonstones. She relaxed as she immersed herself in the work she loved.

Becoming a jewelry designer had been accidental. She'd been majoring in art.

There had been only one piece of jewelry in the window of the shop on College Avenue. A ring. She looked down at her second finger to reassure herself it was still there. A delicate little gold dolphin curved around a chunk of deep green jade held in place with tendrils of yellow and white gold splashed around it like sea foam. She'd loved it from the moment she first laid eyes on it, but it was well beyond her budget as a student. Each day she'd stop by the shop window to reassure herself it was still there; each day she stood and coveted it. Then one day, in its place there was a bracelet. It was a very nice bracelet, beautifully worked, but she was close to tears as she looked at it. Her dolphin was gone.

The shopkeeper, a short plump man who resembled every child's image of Santa Claus, opened the door wide. "Come in, come in," he said, his bushy white beard bobbing and his blue eyes sparkling. "I've been watching you for weeks. You're looking for the dolphin ring. It's still here. I couldn't let anyone else buy it. It was clearly meant for you."

"But I can't begin to pay for it," Caitlin answered. She looked around the shop. The showcases housed one-of-a-kind pieces. Each was a work of art. "They're so beautiful," she breathed. "How do you do this?"

"Come and see," he invited, leading her through to his workshop in the back.

That was the beginning of her three-year apprenticeship with Absalom Klein. Caitlin received her Bachelor of Arts degree from the university, but her real education was in the back room of the little shop on College Avenue.

How she missed his wise council. What would Absalom have done in this situation? What would he have thought about Marie Antoinette's little dragon? The answer came as clearly as if he'd been in the room with her. "It's a piece of French history. It belongs to France. It should not be tangled up in years of court battles. Give it back to the Louvre," Absalom would have said. He always cut through to the quick of the matter.

Aristotle's voice interrupted her reflections. "Breakfast is ready."

Following her nose to the kitchen, Caitlin was astounded at the feast on the table. Cheese soufflé, homemade scones, fried sugared apple slices, jam, coffee.

She inhaled the enticing aromas. "Who did all this?"

Colin raised his hand somewhat sheepishly. "I like to cook."

He stood there, wearing her ruffled calico apron. He had shed his jacket and rolled up his sleeves to reveal broad shoulders and sinewy muscular arms. His torso, freed from its usual concealing layer of baggy tweed, was lean and sleek.

He held a professorship in history, he had lovely blue eyes, he was six foot two, he had a body like Michelangelo's David, and he cooked. Perhaps she'd been a bit hasty in her assessment of him.

Aristotle pulled out a chair for her. "Let's eat before the soufflé falls."

Chapter Six

Buttering the last scone and slathering it with marmalade, Caitlin said, "Okay. I know you two have been scheming behind my back. What do you think we should do?"

"Well…" Colin picked up his coffee mug and then put it back down, untouched. He looked guardedly at Caitlin. "Since you don't want to make the trip, I think I should be the one to return the dragon to the Louvre. So far, the thieves haven't connected it to me. I'm scheduled to make a research trip to France next month. The term is over. I'll change the date of my flight and go now. I'm well known at the Louvre. I'll return the dragon in person. The curator of the historic jewelry collection is a friend of mine. I'll take the dragon to Paris and turn it over to her."

Aristotle added, "That way, you'll be free to work on the Marcus & Pfeiffer collection and I'll be here to look after you."

Caitlin looked from one to the other. "Not on your life! I've been assaulted and robbed, my place of business and my home have been ransacked, all because of this two-inch piece of jewelry. If you think I'm going to let anyone but me take that dragon back to Paris, you're mistaken."

Colin grinned broadly.

Son of a bitch. He'd manipulated her into saying

she'd go. After she'd sworn she wouldn't.

Caitlin shook her head. "I'll need two weeks to finish the designs for the collection and send off the first shipment."

"No problem," Colin said. "So it's settled then? Two weeks from today? The two of us? I'll make the travel arrangements. It should be a quick turnaround. We go to Paris. I telephone my friend and we turn the dragon over to her." He paused. "You don't have to come if you don't want to, Caitlin. I can do it all myself."

Caitlin glared at him. "It's *my* dragon. It was left in *my* shop. If anybody's going to turn it over to the Louvre, it's going to be *me*."

Aristotle spoke for the first time during the heated exchange, his voice resigned. "I'm not about to let Caitlin out of my sight as long as those two men haven't been apprehended. Where she goes, I go." He turned to Caitlin. "I guess you'll have to give me an advance on my Christmas bonus for the airfare."

"Actually," Colin said, "I have enough points..."

"Points?" Caitlin and Aristotle said in unison.

"Well, I'm invited to speak in a lot of places. And they always pay my airfare. And I collect the points. I must have a million of them. Easily enough for the three of us. So no worries on that score. I'll get on it right away. But there could be one problem."

"Problem?" Caitlin and Aristotle chorused.

"There are descriptions of the dragon out there. Interpol is on the alert for it, as are the major customs offices of the world. It might have been easy to smuggle it out of France and into the U.S. six years ago, but to get it back to France with today's beefed up security…"

"And in the meantime, for the next week, we need to keep it safe," Aristotle added.

"I have it in a secure location at the university now. I think we should just leave it there until we're ready to go. But getting it out of the country? That's another problem."

Aristotle snapped his fingers. "Somerset Maugham!"

"You mean the writer? What about him?" Colin looked at Aristotle with interest.

"*The Letter!* It's a short story about an incriminating letter hidden in plain view in a rack of other letters. They made it into a movie twice."

"Of course," Colin laughed. "Brilliant! Caitlin, all you have to do is hide it in plain sight, inside another piece of jewelry." He thought for a moment. "Do it in silver or copper so it won't appear to be particularly valuable."

Aristotle added, "Maybe you could do it with an invisible hinge so the dragon can be easily removed."

Caitlin smiled. "Leave it to me."

While Aristotle stayed on guard duty, Colin drove to his quarters near the university. When he returned, he had a duffle bag of clothes and a box with books and his laptop in it.

"I'll try not to get underfoot. Just go on with your life as if I weren't here."

****

Easier said than done, Caitlin thought. Ignoring Colin in her home was like ignoring a lion in a room full of kittens. He did his best to stay out of the way, but she was all too aware of his very large, very male, presence. Caitlin found she was never alone. She should have been annoyed, but in a way it was endearing he took his responsibility for protecting her so seriously. She was sure his protection was unnecessary. There had been no further searches of her property either in the house or in her shop. Probably the thieves had given up. Still...

Caitlin fell into a daily routine. Life was very different with Colin around. Breakfast was on the table when she came downstairs. He drove her to the shop in the morning and picked her up in the late afternoon. When she went for a run after work, he was always beside her, measuring his steps to hers. She tried not to stare at his muscular legs, his broad shoulders, his strong arms. How could a history professor look like that? It wasn't right.

After her run and shower, she always worked in her studio. Each evening, at eight on the dot, he came to get her.

"Dinner. It's time you stopped work for the day."

Beef in burgundy sauce, roast duck with orange, coq au vin. Caitlin was afraid to get on her scale. But oh! The man could cook!

****

Colin stood at the kitchen counter, absently slicing mushrooms for the veal Cordon Bleu he was preparing for their dinner. This was proving to be much harder than he anticipated. He'd wanted Caitlin the first moment he'd laid eyes on her, standing behind her worktable, showing him stones for his mother's birthday present. That gorgeous mass of hair, pulled back to show her long neck; the tendrils curling around her beautiful Monet face. Her long lithe body with its gentle curves, all right where they should be. Her voice, so low and melodious. What did the French call it? A *coup de foudre*? Love at first sight? Ridiculous. All he knew was he wanted her with an intensity, a fierce longing, he hadn't experienced in many years. He wanted to grab her and kiss her breathless and then take her to bed until she begged for mercy.

And yet, here he was, a guest in her home, in a position where he couldn't touch her. Where he couldn't possibly let her know his feelings for her. It was his responsibility to protect her. To make a move on her under the circumstances would be the worst kind of breach of trust. He couldn't do that.

Colin looked down. He had sliced at least twice as many mushrooms as he needed for dinner. He'd be relieved when this nursemaid role ended and he could begin to show her he cared for her. But what then? She had given him no reason to think she was attracted to him. She treated him the way she treated Aristotle. Like a big brother. His feelings for her were anything but brotherly. Once they were through with Marie Antoinette's little dragon, he'd lay his feelings on the line. He'd court her with every bit of guile in his system until she was his. He didn't even want to contemplate a life without her.

****

After dinner, they sat on the floor in the living room on the ruined cushions, leaning against the wall, with soft jazz on the radio, and talked as they had every evening. This was Colin's favorite time of the day. It seemed natural for him to put his arm around her, for her to rest her head on his shoulder as they talked.

"You have a lovely home here, Caitlin. You said it

was left to you by your parents?"

"Yes. They were killed in an automobile accident when I was eighteen." Caitlin sighed, looking into the past.

"I'm so sorry. It must have been a difficult time for you." Colin tightened his arm around her.

"I'm not sure how I would have managed it if it hadn't been for Absalom."

"Absalom?"

"Absalom Klein, the wonderful man I bought my shop from. He took me on as his apprentice soon after the death of my parents and became, not just a teacher, but a father figure to me. My work with him saved me. I discovered I love creating beautiful things. It absorbs my life and pushes away the loneliness."

She nestled in closer to Colin. "Then Aristotle came along. No one could ask for a better friend."

He inhaled the sweet smell of her hair and imagined running his fingers through its soft curls. He sighed. Not here. Not now. Instead he responded, "I can't imagine how hard it must have been for you, alone at eighteen. I have so much family. Four brothers and three sisters. And an army of aunts and uncles and cousins. And that's just the Irish branch of the Strykers. I also have an aunt and uncle and cousins in Brittany. I used to spend summers with them. Family is big in Ireland. It's the core of our life."

"It must be wonderful." Caitlin yawned and snuggled closer against him. "How'd you learn to cook the way you do?"

"Summers in Brittany. My uncle was *chef de cuisine* in a Michelin-starred restaurant. It may not sound like much here, but it's a big deal in France. He took me to the market with him every morning at dawn to choose the ingredients he'd cook with that night. And then he used me sometimes as a sort of junior grade sous-chef. I felt singled out and important, and I learned to love cooking. I'm afraid from what I've seen, it's an overlooked art in America."

He looked down at Caitlin. She had fallen asleep. He thought of trying to wake her, but settled instead for lifting her up gently into his arms and carrying her upstairs. When he put her into her bed she twined her arms more tightly around him and murmured indistinguishably. With great gentleness he disentangled her arms and brought the covers up over her. He could not resist kissing her on the forehead and whispering, "Good night, my sweet Caitlin."

****

Caitlin frowned as she sat at her worktable. He never made a move. He never even attempted to kiss her. Why? Was she just not his type? Had she only imagined the flash of sexual hunger she had sensed early in their relationship?

Oh, well, she didn't have time for romance in her life at this moment. If her parents' marriage was any example, she wasn't sure she ever wanted a man in her life. It was just as well Colin Stryker wasn't interested.

Somehow her inner protestations didn't quite ring true.

She worked on the Marcus-Pfeiffer collection until her fingers were numb and cramping and her eyes were blurred, and by the end of two weeks, she had most of it completed and sent off to the luxury store. Enough so she could go away for a few days without worrying.

Caitlin invited Aristotle to join them for dinner the

night before they were to leave, with Colin cooking, of course.

When they pushed their chairs back from the table, replete from the last bites of Colin's upside-down plum cake, Caitlin said, "Give me the dragon."

"I'm not sure it's a good idea." Colin shook his head.

"Did you or did you not say we might have trouble with it going through customs?"

"Yes, but…"

"No buts. We can't afford to have this whole crazy scheme sidetracked before we even get on a plane."

"She has a point," Aristotle chimed in. "Give her the dragon, Colin."

Colin reached into the inside pocket of his jacket and handed the small amulet to Caitlin.

"Come with me." She led them into her little workshop. There she picked up a silver dolphin she'd just finished. The dolphin curved as if leaping out of the water, and was suspended from a wide flat silver chain.

"Nice piece." Colin commented. "New?"

"Just finished this afternoon. It needs just a drop or two of silver solder." So saying she laid the sea creature on her worktable and opened it wide. Along the bottom of the piece were tiny invisible hinges. She nestled the dragon in the dolphin and closed it. It was a perfect fit. She seamed the open edge with silver solder. "Voila! No more dragon."

"Brilliant!" Colin approved. "But it looks a little large for you as a piece of jewelry."

Caitlin pursed her lips. "I thought Aristotle could wear it. On him it would look normal."

"Sorry, Caitlin. No can do. I can't wear it. Not with

my dreadlocks and the way I dress. I know they say there's no racial profiling in airport security, but they lie. I'm a Rasta, and I'll be the one they strip search."

"I suspect you're right," Colin agreed. He hesitated before continuing. "Have you completed your oral comprehensive examinations, Aristotle?"

"Sure. Two years ago. I've been working on my dissertation ever since, just taking occasional classes when I thought they might have some relevance to my research."

"Did you wear what you have on now to the examination?"

Aristotle grinned. "Well…no. My supervisor strongly recommended a dark suit and a dress shirt and tie. And I pulled my hair back into a sort of pony tail."

"You still have those clothes?"

"I didn't throw them away, if that's what you mean. But I've never worn them since. I'm saving them for my dissertation defense." He grimaced. "I hate having to put on that kind of show. This is who I am."

Colin studied him for a moment. "Is it? Is this who you are? Rastafari? Do you believe in the sanctity of Haile Selassie? Do you believe the former king of Ethiopia was some kind of god, to be worshiped?"

"Of course not, but—"

"No. I didn't think so. Your hair, your diet, your lifestyle are a sort of gauntlet thrown down to the white majority you have to live with. As an Irishman, I understand all too well. I've thrown a few gauntlets myself. But don't mix up unimportant external symbols with values, which are quite another thing. Choosing to be a vegetarian, choosing not to touch alcohol, they're values. They say something about who you are. But wearing Rasta colors? Being unwilling to tame your hair? Think about it, Aristotle."

"The hair stays. Is this your way of suggesting I put on a suit and tie for this jaunt?"

"No. A tie's unnecessary. But a conservative jacket and jeans might go a long way to making the three of us less obtrusive. And it might even get you through security without a full body search."

Caitlin looked from one to the other. "We're off topic, guys. Who's going to wear the dolphin?"

"No one," Colin answered promptly. "Think about it. That much metal will send off alarm bells for whoever wears it. Then it would have to be taken off and put in a basket where anyone could grab it. No. Do you have one of those jewelry pouches I've seen in stores? The kind with multiple pockets? You can put rings and ear rings and whatever in them and then roll them up and tie them?"

"Sure. I have a couple of them."

"Put the dolphin in one and put several other pieces in with it. Then stick the pouch well down in your handbag. They may do a search, but they're unlikely to single out one piece of jewelry among several."

"We're back to *The Letter*," Aristotle grinned.

"Just so." Colin agreed. "I've booked the limo for noon tomorrow. Can you meet us here at noon, Aristotle? Our flight's at three."

"Sure, no problem."

"Travel light. Nothing but carry-on. I'll have a back pack with a change of clothes and my laptop." Colin turned to Caitlin.

"I've got a back pack. And if I can use your computer I won't have to carry mine." She responded.

****

At noon the next day Caitlin and Colin were ready and waiting for the airport van to come and get them.

Aristotle arrived just as the van pulled up. He had on jeans, a dark sweater, and his suit coat, with his hair pulled back and tied at the nape of his neck. Colin smiled, but refrained from comment.

****

Peering through the high hedge surrounding the vacant house with the For Sale sign, Nic Bisset stubbed out his cigarette on a tree trunk and turned to Jules.

"We've been watching this *ménage á trois* for a week now and nothing's happened. I'm beginning to think that woman doesn't know anything about the dragon."

"I told you not to kill Alain until we had it in our hands. We should have kept him alive until then." Jules Allard was disgusted and tired. The operation had been botched from the first moment. Nic had enjoyed tormenting Alain and, as a result, they now had no idea where the damned dragon was. Someday, his partner's enjoyment of the knife was going to get them both killed.

"He said it was in the shop," Nic insisted, his speech ugly, rasping, closing the subject.

"But it wasn't." Jules' was the voice of reason. "We know that now. And we still don't know where it is. It wasn't in the shop and it wasn't in the house. I'm beginning to think it's lost permanently." He sighed. "I think we should cut our losses and go back to Paris, Nic. There's lots of good pickings still there. With Alain out of the picture, maybe we should take over his line of business."

"Cat burglary? Get real, Jules. Can you see us hanging out with those rich people like he did? Knowing where and when there would be jewelry for the picking. No. That kind of burglary isn't for us. But the Louvre isn't the only museum in the world with jewels. I think we should move on. We're wasting our time here."

"Maybe." Jules squinted through the hedge again. "Were you able to find out who the other big sucker is? The white one with the red hair? Two of them with her day and night. She must be some piece of action!"

"I told you the day he moved in," Nic replied. "I followed him to the university and asked a couple of students about him. He's some professor from Ireland. Stryker. Colin Stryker. A history professor. He can't have anything to do with the dragon. Alain would have given us his name."

"Something's happening!" Jules pulled Nic to the hedge. "Look! They're going someplace, all three of them. An airport van. They're taking a trip. We'd better find out where."

Together they raced to the rental car parked in the driveway of their stakeout house.

Chapter Seven

At the airport, Colin guided them to the first class check-in counter. With no checked bags, they moved quickly through immigration and security. Aristotle made it through in record time.

"I hate to admit it, but you're right. This is the first time I ever got through security without a shakedown." Aristotle grinned. "I like it. It's taking on protective coloration, isn't it? Like the lizards I grew up with in the islands. They were green when they sat on a leaf, but they turned brown on the veranda railing. They don't stop being lizards. They just blend in to the environment instead of fighting it. I think you just taught me a very important lesson, Dr. Stryker."

"My pleasure, Aristotle. Let's wait for the flight in the first class lounge. They'll have food and drink and comfortable chairs. Someone will let us know when our flight's boarding."

"Nice to know how the rich and famous travel," Caitlin quipped.

"My dear," Colin replied, "The rich and famous travel on their own jets. We're just traveling the way most business people do...I might add, at their company's expense."

Settled into a deep leather seat, Caitlin curled up and went promptly to sleep. The long hours of the preceding weeks had taken their toll.

Colin and Aristotle sat sipping orange juice.

"Aristotle's an unusual name," Colin said.

"You mean Aristotle is an unusual name for a black man from a Caribbean island. You should meet the rest of my family. There are my brothers, Euclid, and Plato, and my sisters, Aphrodite and Athena. What can I say? My father was captivated by the Greeks. He taught in our local high school. He was a literate man in love with the ideals of ancient Greece. That is, until he discovered Rastafari. Like many of his Rasta brothers of his time, he believed in the divinity of Haile Selassie. It was heady stuff, a sacred black king directly descended from a lineage dating back to the Old Testament. I know it must seem a bit odd to you. But perhaps you can understand why I cling to some of the outward signs of Rastafari. Not to do so would seem, in some small way, dishonoring my father."

Colin took some time to digest this. "Is your father still living?"

"No. He died five years ago."

"Perhaps you've done your penance long enough. I'm not suggesting you change your beliefs, anything that matters to you. Keep your hair long. Follow your vegetarian diet. Avoid alcohol. But the day is coming soon when you'll be looking for an academic appointment, a tenure track professorship." Colin grinned. "Remember the lizard."

A young woman approached them. "Your plane will be boarding in ten minutes, Dr. Stryker."

"Thank you."

"Caitlin?" Colin brushed her hair back gently back from her face. "Caitlin, wake up. We have to go. The plane is boarding."

Aristotle's eyes widened. Colin was in love with Caitlin. When had that happened?

****

Nic and Jules watched from across the departures hall as the threesome checked in for the Paris flight.

"They've got it. I know they've got it. Somehow they've managed to hide it and now they're taking it back to Paris." Jules ground out the words.

"But why, Jules? They could sell it in the underground here. You know there's always a market. They don't have to take it back to Paris to sell it. It just doesn't make sense." Nic shook his head, baffled.

"They don't intend to sell it. They intend to return it."

"You mean return it to the Louvre? Why would anyone do that?"

Jules glared in annoyance at his partner. "Maybe they're honest? Maybe they don't need the money? Whatever the reason, we have to get on that flight to Paris. We have to stop them before they get to the Louvre."

Resolutely he pulled Nic across the terminal toward the Air France counter. A long line of people pushing their bags along ahead of them snaked their way slowly toward the counter.

"Get out your passport and have it ready. *No! Not that one, imbecile!*" Jules dropped his voice and looked around to make sure no one had heard. "*I told you to destroy that one!*" He grabbed the EU passport out of Nic's hands and buried it deep in the pocket of his coat. "Where's the one I gave you before we left Paris?"

"Right here." Nic pulled out a second passport, this one with a Canadian emblem emblazed on the cover.

"Why do you think I paid 2500 Euros for these new passports? We couldn't have even gotten out of France on our old ones," Jules hissed. "Remember, for purposes of this trip, your name is Francois Dumont and you're from Montreal. And my name is Alfonse Berniet. We are travelling on business. And if anyone asks what business, say 'jewelry.' It's close enough to the truth."

Finally it was their turn.

Jules plunked down a credit card in the name of Alfonse Berniet along with their two passports. "We'd like two seats on the flight leaving for Paris this afternoon."

The agent looked at him with a frown. "Sir, this is a check-in line. To purchase ticket you'll have to go to the ticketing center. It's about halfway down the hall, on the left. Next?"

Swallowing curses, Jules headed in the direction the agent had indicated, Nic hurrying along behind him.

Fortunately there was no line here. "Two tickets for Paris, this afternoon's flight."

The agent studied the screen for a few moments and said, "I'm sorry, sir. That flight is already boarding. And in any case, there are no seats available."

Jules banged his hand on the counter in frustration. "When's the next flight?" he asked.

"On Tuesday," the agent replied. "But I'm not sure we have any seats left on that one either."

"Look, ma'am," Jules tried to keep the desperation out of his voice. "We have to get to Paris. My father is very ill. I must get home."

The agent looked at him with sympathy in her gaze, and turned back to her computer. "You might still get on Icelandic Air. They have a flight via Reykjavik, connecting in Frankfurt with Lufthansa to Paris. I think it's your best bet. It leaves in three hours and they still show some seats. You'll find them down at the end of the international terminal."

The two set off at a run. Three hours later, squeezed into miniscule seats with no leg room, they were on the first of a series of flights that would take twenty-three hours to get to Paris. They swore heartily at the fates that had put them in this position.

"If I ever get my hands on that—" Nic muttered.

"Try not to kill her before we have the dragon," Jules cautioned.

****

Caitlin woke long enough to eat a few bites when the dinner service came, then she went promptly back to sleep, curled up in the seat next to Colin. When the lights were lowered, he pushed his seat back, put his arm around her and pulled her to him. She snuggled into his embrace like a small cat, first stretching and then finding her best position.

He slept little, his imagination on overdrive.

****

They arrived in Paris at noon on a beautiful spring day.

Colin gave the taxi the address of the small hotel on the Left Bank where he always stayed when he was in Paris, on the Rue de Lille, not far from the university, the Sorbonne. He had booked three rooms on the same floor. He and Aristotle were across the hall from one another. Caitlin's room was next to his.

"Paris!" Caitlin breathed, now fully awake. "I can't believe we're here. I want to see everything!"

Colin yawned, standing, key in hand, outside his room door. "I want to call Gabrielle before we do anything else."

"Gabrielle?"

"My curator friend at the Louvre. I promise, once we've disposed of this little charm, we can take a couple of days to see Paris. But I won't feel safe until it's where it belongs, in the museum."

He fit his key into the lock and swung his door open. "Which reminds me, fish it out of your jewelry roll now, Caitlin. I don't want it on or near you. It's brought bad luck to everyone who's ever had it."

"Surely you don't believe in that sort of nonsense, Colin?" Caitlin teased. "A curse on a charm?"

"Caitlin, I'm Irish. We believe in all sorts of superstitious nonsense. Fairies and elves and leprechauns and banshees. And most certainly in the efficacy of curses."

Aristotle laughed out loud. "You have that in common with my people, only with us it's the walking dead and obeah priests who can work love spells or help us take revenge against anyone who's done us wrong."

"Love spells, you say?" Colin looked interested.

Aristotle nodded. "Sure. You ever want any help, just ask."

Caitlin looked from one to the other. "You're both crazy."

"The charm, Caitlin. Please," Colin insisted.

"Oh, very well." She went into her room, leaving the door ajar and dumped her purse upside down on the bed. The little silk jewelry roll came tumbling out along with keys, loose change, lipsticks, tissues, and a number of other small objects. "Here," she said, fishing out the dolphin. "Take it."

"Perhaps I should wear it until we turn it over to your friend," Aristotle suggested.

"Good idea. Let's go into my room and I'll call her now."

Aristotle leaned on the doorjamb and Caitlin perched on Colin's bed while he tried his friend's personal number.

He frowned. "She's not answering. I'll try later. I think we should all take a little rest now. Get over jet lag. Let's meet in Aristotle's room at"—he looked at his watch—"three?"

The others nodded their assent and disappeared into their rooms.

Colin noticed a connecting door between his room and Caitlin's. "Get thee behind me," he muttered under his breath.

****

Caitlin unpacked and put her things in the small armoire, then shed her travel clothes and pulled on the oversized T-shirt she usually slept in and stretched out on her bed.

Five minutes later she realized it was no use. She wasn't in the least sleepy. She'd slept soundly on the plane. She was, she was—

Before she had a chance to change her mind she was off the bed and opening the connecting door.

He was sprawled across the bed, his face turned away from her, his breathing the even tempo of one deeply asleep. She smiled. He slept in the buff. His body was as gorgeous as she'd imagined it. Wide shoulders tapering to narrow waist and lovely tight butt.

All muscles and sinews. There was a faint dusting of red-gold hair on his legs and arms.

When had she first realized she wanted him? She wasn't sure but she thought it was from almost the moment she saw him, standing in her shop, wearing that ridiculous tweed jacket and looking down at her with those incredible blue eyes.

But he seemed not so much uninterested as unaware of her as a woman. Almost insultingly unaware. After one brief flash of sexual hunger she sensed, he'd never made an advance of any kind. He treated her almost like a younger sister. Someone to cherish, to take care of, but not, certainly not, to make love to. He'd spent two weeks in her home. He'd had every opportunity. And nothing had happened. It seemed he didn't want her the way she wanted him.

She sighed and turned to go back to her room.

"Don't go. I'm not sure I can bear it if you go."

She turned slowly.

He was standing by the bed, tension in every line of his body. Behind him a breeze ruffled the curtains at the tall casement windows. The sound of traffic came up, muffled, from the street below.

"I couldn't sleep," she said.

"And so?" The words held immeasurable yearning.

"So, do you want me or don't you?"

He took a ragged breath. "Caitlin, I've wanted you since the moment I first saw you. I wanted you then. I want you now."

Caitlin walked hesitantly toward him, until they stood only inches apart. She could feel the heat emanating from his body, feel the pulsing of his hard erection.

He searched her eyes. "You're sure?"

Caitlin stepped back, pulled the T-shirt over her head and threw it down. "I'm sure. Let's just get on with it."

Abruptly he dropped his hands and took a step back. "No, Caitlin. We won't *just get on with it*. I haven't waited patiently all these weeks just to bang you."

He cupped her face in his hands and kissed her gently. Then he ran his hands down her arms, raising goosebumps in their trail. Cupping her breasts, he rubbed her nipples lightly until they stood in hard peaks.

She squirmed under his touch. "Colin—"

"Shush. Come to bed."

With a shudder, Caitlin sat on the side of the bed.

Colin gently pushed her back. "Turn over. Lie on your stomach."

"What?"

"Caitlin, you're going to have to learn to trust me. Lie on your stomach. I want to love every inch of you."

She had never in her life been so aroused.

He kissed the nape of her neck, soft moist kisses, little nips. With tantalizing slowness he worked his way down her spine to the crease of her buttocks as she writhed and whimpered under him. He cupped the fullness of her bottom in his hands. "You have a gorgeous ass, Caitlin."

"Get on with it," she said through clenched teeth.

"I told you before, Caitlin," he said kissing the back of her knee. "I'm a history professor. We don't know how to 'get on with it.' We tend to be very thorough."

His teasing tone both infuriated and excited her. What in God's name had she unleashed? She ached and writhed with the strain of wanting.

He turned her over on her back and with his hands and mouth he continued his exploration, soft moist kisses tracing her breasts, her belly, and down her legs to her feet.

"You have lovely feet, Caitlin." He knelt and took one in his hand, kissing and licking the sensitive arch.

Her body arched off the bed.

He knelt over her. "Open to me, Caitlin." His agile fingers worked their magic on her. She gasped when he slid down and his lips and tongue caressed. The feel of his soft beard between her legs, against her already over-sensitized flesh was like…like…a shiver rippled through her as she cried her need, her want. Ahhh!

"Good. Now…" He positioned himself over her. Then he was inside her and moving. Moving slowly, every deep plunge sending small shivers of delight through her, each thrust making her cry out. The heat. The unbearable heat. She soared to a shuddering climax as he fell on her with a muffled shout.

At last, reluctantly, they parted a few inches, both breathing heavily. "Are you satisfied, my Caitlin?"

She relaxed and snuggled against him, entwining her legs with his, her head neatly fitted into the hollow between his shoulder and neck. Her arm lay across him. She threaded her fingers through the gold curls on his chest, then let her hand wander lower to the nest of curls and his now limp, harmless…not so harmless. At her touch, he sprang to life again.

"No Caitlin," he mumbled. "Not now. Sleep. I need sleep. More later. I promise."

"Then sleep. I'll wake you at three."

There was no answer except his soft, regular breathing.

Quietly, Caitlin disentangled herself and went back to her room. She stood leaning against the door, ripples of remembered pleasure shooting through her, leaving her shaking. She couldn't let him see her like this. He mustn't know how deeply he had affected her. It had never been like this. There had been a couple of fumbling encounters in university, entered into more from curiosity than desire. "It will be better next time," the boy had said after the hasty, messy taking of her virginity. It hadn't been. Since then she had never wanted to be with anyone. She hadn't seen much point to it.

Colin had brought her to the edge of reason, where nothing existed but pleasure. He had her spinning out of control.

Still, she was the one who had pulled him into bed. She was the one who instigated the sex. She'd thought she was playing with a house cat, and she'd ended up with a tiger. Now, what was she going to do with him?

She wanted more. She knew she'd come to his bed again the first time he asked her. And again and again. She wanted him, she needed him as she'd never imagined she could need a man. She hated the feeling. She, who had always been in control of her own life, in control since she was eighteen.

He was a dangerous man. If she wasn't careful, he'd derail her carefully planned and constructed life. Emotional entanglements weren't easy for her, ever, but to be in love with an insane Irishman who spent half his life trotting around the globe? What about her work, her hard-earned career?

But, oh, she did want him. She wanted nothing more than to be in his bed, in his arms. What was she going to do about that?

****

Eyes closed, Colin was aware of her leaving his arms. An almost visceral pain shot through him when she separated herself from him. He wanted to keep her here in his bed and make love to her again and again, until there was nothing left but their bones. His wanting was primitive, unreasonable. He had never experienced anything like it in his life before. She was his and she'd better damn well accept it. There would be no other men for her now or ever, only him. And he'd see to it she was happy with the arrangement, satisfied and happy. He knew now he could do so, even exhausted as he had been when she came into his room. She'd brought him to fever pitch just standing there. What would it be like to make love to her when he was rested? It might well kill them both. He was going to have to exercise some control. He couldn't just jump her every time she was near, could he?

No family. She had no family. Who could he even ask for her hand? Who could guide him so she wouldn't bolt, colt-like, in the face of his passion? How could she know so little about sex, about arousal?

Exhausted, he slept, dreaming of her moving under him, and awoke drenched in sweat and with a painfully hard erection. He took a cold shower and dressed. Time to meet with Aristotle and Caitlin.

Chapter Eight

Aristotle glanced at his watch. Three, they'd said, and it was now twenty after.

Colin knocked briefly and walked in. "Sorry I'm late. I guess I fell asleep." He didn't meet Aristotle's eyes. He crossed the room and sat in the chair by the window, looking at the street below, avoiding Aristotle's contemplation. "We need to talk later."

Aristotle considered him. He didn't look like he'd been sleeping. Not alone, anyway. "Yes. I think we do need to talk," he replied, giving Colin a hard look. If he did anything to hurt Caitlin...

Caitlin came in. Her lips were swollen, and her skin had that unmistakable luminescent, after-sex glow. "Sorry," she said to Aristotle, as she perched on the bed, not looking at either Aristotle or Colin.

Okay, that's how it is, Aristotle thought. *Let's see how long it takes one of them to level with me.*

"I'll try Gabrielle again." Colin pulled out his phone a punched in the number. On the other end, an answering machine clicked in. "Gabrielle, it's Colin. I'm in Paris and I need to see you urgently. Call me as soon as you get this message."

He frowned. "It's unlike her not to answer her private number, even at work. Maybe I should call her office at the Louvre. It could be she's out of town." He dialed another number from memory.

A female voice answered. "Special Collections, The Louvre, how may I redirect your call?"

"This is Professor Stryker calling. Could you put me through to Dr. Colbert, please?"

There was a moment's silence on the other end of the line. Then, "I'm afraid Dr. Colbert is no longer with us. Is there someone else to whom we could direct your enquiry? Dr. Pierre Lamont is now curator of the antique and royal jewelry collection."

"No. No thank you."

Colin looked at the others in shock. "She's not there. She's not at the Louvre. She's been replaced... by a man, I might add, who used to be her assistant, and for whom as a scientist, she had very little respect. What's going on?"

Aristotle sighed. "There goes our neat little plan of handing the dragon over to your curator friend."

Colin glanced at him. "True. But at this moment I'm more worried about Gabrielle than I am about the dragon. What could have gone wrong? I saw her only..." He paused. "I guess it's been longer than I realized. More than five years ago. But there was no talk of her leaving her job then."

For the first time, Caitlin spoke. "Is she very pretty, this Gabrielle of yours?"

Colin frowned. "No. I wouldn't call her pretty...stunningly beautiful, perhaps, but not pretty. We've been very close for many years." A teasing smile twitched at the corner of his mouth.

"I see." Caitlin glowered at him and lapsed into silence.

Aristotle looked from one to the other. Caitlin looked like she might blow up at any moment. Colin would have to learn she didn't take well to teasing.

Colin's phone rang.

"Thank God it's you." Colin's voice reflected his relief. "What's going on? I called the museum…Yes, of course I can come. Immediately…the same address? Good. I have two friends with me. I'll explain everything when we get there."

"So you know her address. Stayed there from time to time, have you?" Caitlin's tone was edged with ice.

"Yes," Colin answered mildly. "Actually I've stayed there a number of times. Gabrielle and I have been close friends for many years."

In the taxi, Colin was quiet, Aristotle sat between the two like a parent between two quarrelsome children, while Caitlin looked out the window in frozen silence.

****

The apartment house dated from the late nineteenth century and was floridly decorated in the style that flourished as art nouveau.

"This building is under the protection of the Ministry of Culture," Colin said. "Those sculptures on the façade are museum worthy."

"Indeed?" Caitlin looked at the ornate entranceway. "A bit fussy for my taste." But in one corner of her mind she was already translating the lines into jewelry. Copper, perhaps with…

Colin entered a series of numbers into the key pad beside the door and it swung open.

Across a black and white marble-floored foyer, they entered an ornate wrought iron and polished brass lift with barely space for the three of them. It rose sedately to the fifth floor.

"It's a bitch when this elevator isn't working,

which is about half the time," Colin said. "I've suggested to Gabrielle more than once she should consider leaving this mausoleum for a place with more modern conveniences, but she's a very hard-headed woman."

"It appears you specialize in hard-headed women," Aristotle muttered.

"What's that supposed to mean?" Caitlin spat out.

The lift came to a clunking halt at the fifth floor. Colin slid the door open and they exited to another marble-floored foyer with only two doors. Colin headed straight to the one on the right, the front of the house and, ignoring the buzzer, rapped with his knuckles, three times in quick succession on the door.

"A special signal to let her know it's you?" Caitlin asked sweetly.

"Yes. There have been times in her life when not every visitor was welcome," he answered.

The door swung wide and a tall slender woman threw her arms around Colin and kissed him, first on one cheek and then on the other. "My darling Colin. It has been much too long. Come in, come in. And introduce me to your friends."

Caitlin stood in the entranceway, glued to the spot. The woman was indeed beautiful, stunning. She was also sixty, if she was a day. Positively ancient. She'd get Colin for this, for allowing her to think…

"Caitlin, Aristotle," he was saying, "This is my oldest and dearest friend, Gabrielle Colbert. Gabrielle was one of my teachers when I was a feckless youth at the Sorbonne."

The relief flooding through Caitlin left her weak. She was a friend, just a friend, not a former lover. There must have been former lovers. No man could make love like that without practice. Lots of practice. But Gabrielle wasn't one of them. The mere thought of the women he must have loved before her filled her with pain.

"Caitlin?" Colin took her arm and led her to a chair. His touch scorched her. She had to stop thinking about him in bed with her.

Aristotle and Gabrielle were laughing together over something she had missed. She shook her head and brought herself to the present.

"And so you see," Aristotle said, "we were counting on your position in the Louvre to get us out of this mess."

"But I don't understand. What is this *mess*?"

"First, Gabrielle," Colin intervened, "what happened to you? I don't buy you decided to retire. You always said they'd have to take you out feet first."

Gabrielle stood. "I think we'd better have some wine to go with my story. Colin, would you please bring us a bottle and some glasses, while I put together a little tray with some cheese and grapes? I think there's a Beaujolais Nouveau in the wine rack."

With the ease of familiarity, Colin disappeared into the kitchen and returned bearing the bottle of light young red wine and four glasses. Gabrielle followed with a plate containing a soft white brie, a creamy chèvre, and a wedge of Roquefort. A long French loaf and a sharp knife were beside them, on a wooden cutting board.

Caitlin realized she was very, very hungry. She sliced off a chunk of bread and slathered it with the brie. The others followed suit.

Colin raised his glass. "To friends, old and new, absent and present." He took a sip. "Gabrielle you've always had excellent taste in wine. But no more stalling. It's time to level with me. What happened?

"I hate to talk about it. Even to think about it. I've done everything I can to put it behind me. I must if I'm to enjoy the remainder of my life. Nothing's to be gained by rehashing it.

"Gabrielle..."

Caitlin recognized the tone of voice. When Colin spoke that way, people obeyed him.

"Oh, very well!" Gabrielle took a deep breath. "I can see you're not going to leave me in peace until I tell you. To make a long story short, my assistant..."

"Pierre Lamont? The one you always referred to behind his back as 'the weasel'?"

"One and the same. I was caught between two men who really despised me. My so-called assistant, who always thought he should have my job, and the director who thought women had no place in the museum world, and was always ready to believe the worst of me. I walked a fine balance between the two of them for years. I guess in the end, Pierre just got tired of waiting for me to retire. He framed me. It was a crude and obvious frame. He said the thieves had to have had someone inside, an accomplice who was in a position to disable the security system for that wing of the museum, and he pointed the finger at me, saying he had seen me slipping into the room only moments before. He also accused me of enabling the third thief to get away. The director was all too willing to believe him. These unsubstantiated accusations were made, and in the end the director offered me the choice of retiring with full benefits or being dragged through a court case and possibly losing everything. If I'd been younger I might have fought them, but as it was...I simply wasn't up to it. I was tired of the maneuvering and the politics. I decided to get out while I was still young enough to enjoy my life."

Colin raised his eyebrows. "But Gabrielle, if the robbery was dependent on someone disabling the security system, someone else must have done it. Haven't you wondered who?"

"Of course I have, *cheri*. But it could have been anyone. A dozen people had access to the security codes, including even the director. What could I do?" She sat back and took a sip of her wine, savoring it. "But you said you needed my help? Perhaps I can do something. I still have no little influence in the museum world."

Colin took a deep breath. "How well do you remember the actual theft six years ago?"

"I only wish I could forget it. The thieves managed to get into the main showcase and get their hands on some very valuable pieces."

Caitlin had been following the discourse intently. She spoke for the first time. "But it didn't go down as planned, did it? Someone informed the police and they were there waiting. Did you see the man who got away with Marie Antoinette's amulet? Alain Tremont?" It was strange to refer to him by that name even now.

Gabrielle was silent for what seemed an eternity. Then she sighed and looked directly at Caitlin. "As a matter of fact I did. The other two appeared be thugs, truly low-lifes, but the third man was cut of a different cloth. He was most attractive, a gentleman. He blew me a kiss as he disappeared with Marie Antoinette's little trinket." She gave a bitter laugh. "The place was swarming with police and he just walked out."

Caitlin shook her head. "He died for that 'trinket,'" she said. "He was murdered horribly by his former associates."

Gabrielle went pale, swayed, and closed her eyes. "Oh, no." She took a ragged breath and sat down abruptly. For a brief moment Caitlin thought she was going to faint. Then she rallied. "That anyone should be killed for such a reason. Marie Antoinette's little dragon has a bloody history. Perhaps it should stay lost."

Aristotle spoke. "It's too late for that. We have it here with us. And we need your help to get it back into the Louvre."

"*Mon Dieu!* I suppose I could introduce you to Pierre or, perhaps better, to the director, but..."

Colin finished her thought. "You were under suspicion of theft once. To return a stolen object now might make things even worse for you."

"You can imagine the scene. They'd doubtless accuse me of having stolen it in the first place."

"So the problem has changed," Aristotle said. "We now have to get the dragon back to its proper resting place without anyone knowing until it's safely restored to the collection. And there can't be any connection back to you."

"But," Caitlin interjected, "it seems someone in the museum staff isn't to be trusted. If we restore the dragon to the collection, what's to keep it from simply disappearing again? Isn't that so, Colin?"

Colin was standing at the window overlooking the

busy street below, his hands clasped behind his back, his head down in thought.

"Colin?" Caitlin repeated.

He turned to face them, smiling. "I think I know how we can do it. But we'll need lots of publicity about its return. Gabrielle, who do you know in the world of art journalism?

Gabrielle paused for a moment. "Newspaper or magazine?"

"Newspaper."

"Newspaper, Jacques Gilbert. He's the fine arts editor for *le Monde*."

"Can he be discreet?"

"Certainly, if I ask him to."

"We'll give him an exclusive, the whole story, when the time comes, photos, the works. But not yet. I have some things to put in place first. Somehow we have to discover who the inside man was. We need to clear your name, Gabrielle. Even if you never want to work as a curator again, we need to clear your name."

Tears came to Gabrielle's eyes. She wiped them away with her hand. "Thank you, *mon cher ami*, but I am content in my retirement. Perhaps we should—how do you say in English?—*Let sleeping dogs lie*."

Caitlin studied Gabrielle. She didn't seem particularly enthusiastic about a possible foray into the events surrounding the robbery five years ago. Why would that be? She glanced at Colin. He appeared oblivious to Gabrielle's lack of enthusiasm.

The door opened and a young woman came bursting in, then stopped short. "*Pardon, maman, je ne savais pas que tu attendiez des gens.* I didn't know you had company." Then she saw Colin and threw herself into his arms. *"Colin, tu ne m'a pas dit que tu venais!"*

Caitlin drew in a sharp breath. Now who was this, and what was she to Colin?

Colin laughed and swung the young woman in a circle. "Celine! I thought you were in working for a jewelry designer in Nice!"

"I was. But I'm in Paris now. I'm my company's Paris rep. It's my job to sell to the high fashion houses. We're in hopes they'll use some of our pieces in their fall shows."

Turning to Caitlin and Aristotle, Colin introduced the newcomer to them. "This little piece of mischief is Gabrielle's daughter, Celine. I've known her since she was a babe in arms." He smiled affectionately down at the young woman standing beside him. "Celine, I'd like you to meet my friends from America, Caitlin Abernathy and Aristotle Jones."

Caitlin managed a cool *"Enchantée"* to the new arrival, studying her through narrowed eyes. She seemed almost child-like, although she had decidedly un-child-like curves. Small and delicate looking, she had a pixie face, pointed chin, huge dark eyes, and short straight dark hair enlivened with a bright purple streak. Her skin was the color of café au lait. What was she to Colin? She seemed on very familiar terms with him.

"Celine is my goddaughter," Colin explained.

Caitlin drew a relieved breath. Was she so far gone as to be jealous of this child? Yes. The answer came as a shock. She had never cared enough about any man to be jealous. It was not a comfortable feeling. She didn't want to feel this way. So insecure, so needy. What had Colin done to her? She turned to Aristotle. He always knew how to help her when she was lost.

But Aristotle was having problems of his own. Caitlin had never known Aristotle to be at a loss for words in any situation, but he was staring at Celine, tongue-tied. What was going on?

He finally found his voice. He spoke very formally in Celine's own language. *"Ravi de vous rencontrer."*

"You speak French?" Celine turned her full attention on Aristotle.

"French was my first language. My mother was from Martinique. Of course, it wasn't Parisian French we spoke, but I've taken some language courses since. They were required for my degrees."

Caitlin had known Aristotle for five years, and he'd never mentioned his mother spoke French. In fact, he'd rarely said anything about his life in the Caribbean before he came to Berkeley.

"My father was from the French Caribbean islands also, or so I've been told…" the young woman continued. "You speak French very well. With almost no accent." Celine turned to her mother. "So what's going on, *maman*? You all have the appearance of hatching up a plot!"

Gabrielle laughed. "I suppose we are."

Colin asked Celine, "You still have friends at the Sorbonne?"

"Mais oui, of course."

"We may have need of your help later. I'll let you know."

"But what is this about?"

"The short version is we want to reinstate your mother's position at the Louvre while at the same time unmasking the person inside the museum who was responsible for both a theft and for her dismissal."

Colin paused. "Then we need to return a valuable item to the collection, while avoiding some rather nasty characters who are wanted for murder and arson."

Celine's eyes widened as she listened. "Have you any idea how you're going to do this?"

Colin sighed. "Not a clue. But I'm sure something will come to me."

Aristotle chimed in. "Who stood to gain from your mother's dismissal? The man who got your mother's job. Who had access to the security system? The man who got your mother's job. It looks pretty straightforward to me. We just have to trap Pierre Lamont somehow into giving himself away."

Gabrielle sighed. "I wish it were that simple."

Throughout the exchange, Caitlin hadn't taken her eyes off Gabrielle. The curator knew more than she was telling. What was she concealing?

The three decided to walk back to their hotel. It was not far, and they all needed the fresh air and exercise.

Colin peered ahead. "I remember a little café in the next block. Up for some dinner?"

They sat outside under a striped awning and ate chicken stewed in a rich red sauce accompanied by a rough red wine and crusty rolls.

Caitlin took a huge bite of hers and closed her eyes, savoring the flavors.

"I used to eat here when I was a student at the Sorbonne, and then later when I was a visiting professor." Colin took a sip of his wine. "I never quite got used to the French habit of taking a three-hour lunch, eating a huge meal in the middle of the day. I used to eat a sandwich at my desk for lunch, then have my dinner in the evening, here. "

As they approached their hotel sometime later, Colin touched Aristotle's arm. "I'd like to speak with you," he said quietly. "Your room?"

Aristotle nodded.

"I need to go to bed," Caitlin announced. "I think jet lag has caught up with me."

The two men saw her to her door and then retreated to Aristotle's room. Aristotle propped up on the bed against the pillows.

Colin took the only chair in the room, eased his shoes off, rubbed his feet for a moment and then crossed them on the bed. He let his breath out in a long sigh. "I didn't mean to let it happen. Not that way."

Aristotle gave a non-committal "mmm."

"She came into my room. You have to understand. I've been trying to keep from jumpin' her since the day I first met her, in the shop. And then all the time at her house when I was responsible for keepin' her safe, I never touched her. She drove me nearly crazy. But I knew it would be wrong when I was charged with protectin' her…"

He took a deep, shaky breath. "Then this morning she came into my room wearing next to nothing. Wanting me. Asking me to love her. I couldn't help myself. I'm crazy in love with her."

Aristotle frowned. "Of course, I could just knock your socks off. We could get into a knock-down drag-out fight. Is that why you're here? Is that what you want?"

Colin's eyebrows shot up. "No. Of course not. As far as I can see, you're the only family Caitlin has. I want you to know my intentions are honorable."

Aristotle threw back his head and laughed. The laughter rolled up deep and resonant and long.

Colin looked at him, puzzled. "What's so funny? I'm just tryin' to do the right thing."

When Aristotle had himself under control, he wiped his eyes and said, "Don't ever tell Caitlin what you just said to me. I can't even begin to imagine the explosion if she ever found out you and I were sitting here together planning her future."

"But sure an' you care what happens to her?"

"You bet I care what happens to her. If you hurt her I'd be obliged to break every bone in your body."

"I'm not thinkin' to hurt her. I'm thinkin' to marry her. That is, if she'll have me."

"Colin, I don't know how it's done in Ireland, but in America, love and marriage are strictly the concern of the two people involved. Relatives are *told*, not asked."

"I'm not so sure it's any different in Ireland today. It's been eighteen years since I courted a woman. And I asked her father's permission."

"Eighteen years! Are you telling me in eighteen years you have never…"

"I'm not sayin' I havna' been with a few women. I'm not a monk. But there has been no one important in my life, no one I've cared for since Elizabeth. We were engaged to be married. It didn't end well."

Aristotle was silent for a few moments. "I see."

"Is Caitlin too young for me, Aristotle? I worry I may be too old for her. I'm 39. She's so young and inexperienced."

"She's 28. It's not a significant age difference. But I believe her experience with men has been pretty limited, at least in the time I've known her. She's been too busy building a career to have much of a life."

"I'm asking you then as a friend. Do you think I should ask her to marry me?"

"Not yet." Aristotle answered. "In fact, if you're smart, you'll wait and let her ask you. Caitlin likes to be in charge."

"Not always…" Colin grinned a self-satisfied grin. "No. Not always. But I take your point. I'll see if I can make her think it's all her idea."

"Good plan. Now go and get some sleep. We'll reconvene in the morning."

****

Two tired, disheveled men took a taxi from Charles de Gaulle Airport to their small flat in the Marais District. As they climbed the stairs to the fifth floor Nic muttered, "Sleep. I need sleep. If I never see another plane it will be too soon." He fitted his key into the lock and swung the door wide.

Jules followed him in and dumped his bag on the floor. "Good to be home. We'll try to find them once we've had some sleep."

"Why can't you just let it go, Jules? They don't have the dragon. Alain probably broke it up and got rid of the stones years ago. It's a wild goose chase."

"Then why are they in Paris?" Jules went through to the kitchen and poured himself a stiff drink. He said over his shoulder, "They've got the amulet and I intend to get it before they give it back to the Louvre."

"Don't be stupid. Why would anyone give away something that valuable?"

Jules gave a short, humorless laugh. "Maybe because they're honest?"

Nic flopped down in a much worn brown chair beside a dirt-caked window and sighed. "I don't know why they're here, but I don't believe they have the dragon. It's time to call it quits. We need to find another mark soon. We've already spent too much time and money chasing this phantom. We haven't made any money since that quick job in Cannes. Our cash is running low."

Jules took a deep drink of his brandy. "We just need to get their full attention. And I know how we can do it."

"Whatever you say, Jules." Nic took his ever-present knife out of his pocket and caressed it lovingly. His smile would have frightened anyone but Jules.

Chapter Nine

It was seven o'clock in the morning and Caitlin was wide awake. Colin was still sleeping deeply beside her, one arm thrown over her, possessing her even as he slept. He slept on his stomach, his flaming hair disordered against the pillow. She carefully disengaged herself and stood looking down at him. He was heavy when he fell on her after his climax. But how she loved the feel of him on her, in her. It almost frightened her the way he could bring her to blind passion so easily.

She shook her head. Coffee. She needed coffee. She eased the connecting door open quietly so as not to awaken him. Her jeans and a shirt were in a rumpled heap the floor where she'd discarded them last night.

She shivered remembering the urgency of his lovemaking. Was he in love with her? He hadn't said so.

Was she in love with him? She considered the possibility. No. She couldn't be. She'd only known him for a few weeks. It was just twenty-four hours since she had opened the door between their rooms and taken that fateful step into his room, wanting…wanting what? She wasn't sure what impulse made her go to his room or what she had wanted. It certainly wasn't the shattering, soul-searing experience that followed.

And then, last night. He had come into her room and wordlessly kissed her breathless. She remembered him pulling her clothes off in frantic haste, dropping them where she stood. Picking her up as if she were weightless, taking her through to his room, to his bed.

She shivered as she relived what followed. She'd never been so helpless in her life, sensation following sensation. How had he learned to make love like that? How many women had there been in his life before her? The thought intruded painfully, how many would there be after? She shook her head to chase the thought away. A shower. A cold shower should do it.

As she dressed, she thought about how Aristotle and Colin had watched over her during the last weeks. She'd had virtually no freedom of movement. No time just to be alone. One or the other of them was always with her. But Berkeley and its dangers were 10,000 miles away. Nic Bisset and Jules Allard would have no way of knowing they were in Paris. Here, it would surely be safe to be alone, at least for a little while.

Twenty minutes later, she was running down the stairs encircling the tiny wrought-iron lift. She dropped her key at the concierge desk. No one was in sight.

Caitlin stepped out of the door into the bright sunlight of morning in Paris. *Paris.* She'd wanted to come here since she was a teenager. The Eiffel Tower, the Louvre, Montmartre, the broad boulevards, the Champs-Élysées, Notre Dame and Sacré Coeur—

In front of her was a narrow street bordered with trees, their new leaves announcing the imminent arrival of spring. Cars were parked haphazardly on both sides, leaving only one lane for traffic. She laughed aloud as a taxi and a black Peugeot negotiated to see which would back up. The taxi won.

She saw the blue and white striped awning of a

café down the street, at the corner, and headed for it.

"*Bonjour, Monsieur. Un café complét, s'il vous plait,*" she told the black-aproned waiter, hoping he would understand her high school French.

She must have got it right because a few minutes later he arrived back at her table with a pot of steaming coffee, a pitcher of hot foaming milk, a large cup and saucer and a croissant.

She poured the coffee and hot milk into the cup simultaneously, feeling very Parisian as she did so.

She lingered over her breakfast. It was the first time in weeks she hadn't been in the company of one or the other of her two self-appointed guardians. Perhaps they wouldn't miss her for an hour or so. She felt gloriously alive and free, and she wanted some time alone to savor this beautiful city. She pulled out her pocket map. She was on the Left Bank, across the river from the Tuileries Gardens and the Louvre. Crossing the busy street to the sidewalk paralleling the river, the Seine, she headed toward the Pont Alexandre.

The bridge took her breath away. She stood and gazed in wonder. She'd seen pictures of it but the reality was unbelievable. It looked like a wedding cake, with wrought iron wreaths strung along the lower part and fancy lighting standards like old-fashioned candelabra, each with five lights. But the most stunning of the decorations were the gold horses and their accompanying warrior women. It was so overdone, so brilliant, so French! And, unfortunately so full of cars. She glanced to her right and saw a walking bridge a short way down the river. Much better. She strolled along, feasting her eyes on the river traffic, the barges, the boats filled with sightseers, a multitude of smaller craft. It was a lively scene.

A half hour later, she found herself in front of the Louvre, gazing up at the huge glass pyramid marking its entrance. So this is where her little dragon once lived. She crossed her fingers. And with any luck would live again.

She glanced at her watch and sighed. Colin and Aristotle would be up by now and would be wondering where she was. She'd best get back.

With a last longing look at the Tuileries, the beautiful park stretching so invitingly in front of the Louvre, she resolutely turned back toward the bridge and the Left Bank.

She was only a few steps from the hotel when a car pulled up beside her. Jules Allard got out, blocking her way to the hotel. What? She turned and ran. His footsteps pounded after her, closing the distance. She shouted, "*Au secours*! Help! Police!" The street was empty of pedestrians. Rough hands seized her from behind in a fierce grip. She tried to scream but his hand covered her mouth brutally, grinding her lips across her teeth, covering her nose, making it difficult to breathe. His other arm came around her waist and he pulled her backwards, toward the waiting car. Her heart pounded as she struggled in his fierce grip.

"Bitch," he said, "you want to live, you cooperate."

Caitlin forced herself to go limp, as if she had fainted, her lead lolling, her arms dangling at her sides. His grasp loosened as he half dragged, half carried, her dead weight toward the car. More focused on keeping her upright than on keeping her restrained, his grip on her slackened. Caitlin twisted her body out of his embrace, and using the side of her hand to deliver a sharp blow to the base of his nose, she shoved her knee into his groin. He grunted and doubled over in pain, his nose gushing blood. She broke loose and ran toward the busy intersection, where she could see people, find help.

Too late. They were on her again, the two men she had last seen in Berkeley. Terror-stricken, she fought frantically, arms pummeling, legs kicking, opening her mouth to scream. A sharp jab pierced her arm. Her world went black.

She came to slowly. It was dark, almost suffocating in her small coffin-like enclosure. Fighting down her initial panic, she took several deep breaths and twisted her head to see where she was. It was a very cramped space—the trunk of a moving car. A horrible smelly blanket was wrapped around her. She wriggled her head and arms out of it. That was better.

She could feel every bump in the road as the car stopped and started in city traffic. At least they hadn't bound and gagged her. They hadn't had time for that. Could she kick and scream to attract attention the next time they stopped for a light? She positioned herself to kick at the lid of the trunk, but only succeeded in hurting her ankle and in making herself even more uncomfortable. No one would be likely to hear her scream above the din of the surrounding traffic.

She'd just have to wait for her chance when they came to get her out of the trunk. A lot of good that police course in self-defense had done her. They hadn't covered what to do when there were *two* assailants, or when they injected some sort of knock-out drug into their victim.

Now they were on a smoother road and the car was

picking up speed. A highway of some kind? Where were they taking her? What did they want of her? The answer came sickeningly. The dragon, of course. If they had her, they could bargain for the dragon. She loosened the blanket a bit more by pushing with her elbows and knees until it was under her, not wrapped around her. Good. She had some freedom now. It was a bit more comfortable. She'd have to be ready when they came to get her out. She flexed her muscles, moving her arms, her legs. She might well have only one chance to get away from them.

****

Aristotle was returning from his morning run. He was a block from the hotel when he saw two men dumping Caitlin's unconscious body into the trunk of their car.

"*Au secours*! Help! Somebody stop that car!" He ran, looking around frantically for assistance. A young man was dismounting his motorbike, getting ready to secure it to a parking stand.

"Sorry!" Aristotle said, grabbing the handlebars from the startled owner. "You'll get it back," he called over his shoulder as he revved up the motor and headed off in the direction the silver Citroën had just taken. Weaving in and out of increasing rush hour traffic, he fixed his eyes on the vehicle now a block and a half ahead of him. The car made a sharp right turn, heading south. He pushed the little bike to the limit, maneuvering dangerously around cars and trucks, ignoring lights, struggling to keep the Citroën in view.

At the Quai de Bercy, the Citroën shot up the ramp to the Boulevard Périphérique, the ring road around Paris. From there they could be going anywhere,

Aristotle thought despairingly. How much gas did the bike have? He glanced down. Good. It was almost full. If only he could keep up with them. Luckily the traffic here was heavy. The Citroën wasn't able to travel much faster than he could. He had the advantage of being able to slip between the cars. Should he attempt to overtake them? If he could create a major scene, a sufficient traffic jam, perhaps the police would arrive and help.

No. It was too chancy. He was unarmed and there were two of them, both probably with guns, and they had Caitlin as hostage. He couldn't risk her life. At this point, he could only keep them in his sights.

Traffic slowed and Aristotle pulled out his mobile to call Colin. He wasted no time on explanations. "Rent the fastest vehicle you can and head south. They've got Caitlin. I'm following their car. Follow the signs for Orly. And alert the police. I haven't been able to get close enough to see their license plate yet. I'll let you know when I do. It's a silver Citroën." He didn't wait for a response.

They were passing the Orly exit on E-50. Where in God's name were they taking her?

Four hours later, after more twists and turns than he could count, gas running dangerously low, Aristotle followed them off the highway onto a country road in Brittany. He kept several cars between him and his prey. It wouldn't do for them to realize he was on their tail. The bike sputtered and came to a stop, almost spilling him in the process. Aristotle swore under his breath. Out of gas. He would have to leave the bike here and find a petrol station. He headed at a trot down the two-lane road where the car he was following had disappeared.

116

Ten minutes later he came to a roundabout. Three roads leading off it. Which one had they taken? He banged his fist against the road sign in frustration. To come this far only to lose them! At least he'd gotten close enough to get their license number about an hour ago. He'd call Colin with it. Colin must have alerted the police by now.

****

Colin was red in the face and close to total meltdown as the policeman at the front desk in the station said, "But, *bien sûr*, Monsieur, I don't know what you think we can do. A friend of yours reported to you your *petite amie* got into a car with two men, and then your friend stole a motorcycle on the rue de Lille, to follow them. You did not see this supposed abduction. The lady may well have chosen to go with friends for a little excursion. We have, however, received the report of motorcycle stolen on the rue de Lille, and we've issued a warning for the traffic police to be on the look-out for it. As to the young lady, Monsieur, you must know we cannot control with whom she chooses to take a ride?"

"But I tell you she didn't *choose!*" Colin shouted in frustration. "She was abducted. She was taken against her will!"

"Colin!" a familiar voice boomed behind him. "What brings you here?"

The officer looked up from his desk. "Bonjour, André. We weren't expecting you back today."

Colin turned to see his old school friend, André Bergère, an *agent infiltré*, an undercover cop, with the Paris police.

"André! Thank God you're here! Please, you have

to help me. We're in terrible trouble."

"What you doing in Paris? Last I heard you were on your way to California for a year." Colin's friend embraced him and bussed him on both cheeks in the French manner. "It's good to see you. You're having a little problem? Come through to my office."

To the officer at the desk, he said, "I'll take care of this, Honoré."

Once seated in André's small office, Colin forced himself to stem his rising panic and order his chaotic thoughts. His friend would help. "You know the names Nic Bisset and Jules Allard?"

André grimaced. "And Alain Tremont. The one who got away. They're not names I'm likely to forget. I was assigned to the case. It wasn't my finest hour. I'm the one who originally arrested Tremont with his hands full of somebody else's diamonds. I persuaded him he could get a shorter sentence by turning informant. He agreed and helped me set up a scheme to trap Allard and Bisset in the attempted Louvre heist. It didn't go as planned, although we did retrieve all but one piece of the stolen jewels and managed to put two of the three away for a while."

"Well, Bisset and Allard are out now. They're wanted in the U.S. on charges of arson and murder, and they've abducted my fiancée."

"Your fiancée?"

Colin waved the inconsequential half-truth away. "Well, she doesn't know it yet, but I'm going to marry her if I can keep her alive. André, she's in grave danger. And it's my fault. If I hadn't hatched up this crazy scheme…Please help me. I'll explain everything later, but the last I heard, she was in the boot of a silver gray

Citroën, headed west on the Boulevard Périphérique past the Orly exit onto E50. A friend of ours is following them on a stolen motorcycle."

Colin's mobile phone rang. "Slow down, Aristotle. I can't understand you. You have their license number?" Colin jotted it down and showed it to André.

"What? Your bike ran out of gas and you lost them? Tell me where you are." He listened as Aristotle read the direction signs to him. "A roundabout on N 164? Hold on."

André said, "N 164's in Brittany. Why would they take her to Brittany?" He tapped information into his computer. "Allard is from Brittany. Somewhere in the Concarneau area. I'll call my colleagues there to see to it a bulletin is put out immediately to apprehend Bisset and Allard, to approach them as armed and dangerous, and to be aware they have a hostage." He stood and left the room.

Back on the phone with Aristotle, Colin said, "It looks like they may be headed to Concarneau. If you can beg, borrow, or steal wheels, or hitch a ride, meet us there. I'll be in touch."

André returned. "Done," he said. "The police in the Concarneau area will be on the look-out for them."

Colin paced the small room. "I need to find them, André. I can't just leave it in the hands of the police. God knows what those two might do to Caitlin…"

"My Peugeot is just outside and I still have a few days leave left. Let's go. You can fill me in as we go."

****

Caitlin woke with a start. She must have dozed off. How could that have happened? Perhaps the aftereffect of the shot they'd given her? She had a pounding headache and her mouth was so dry she couldn't even swallow. And she desperately needed to pee. She ached in every muscle and joint after bouncing along in this cramped position for what seemed like half a lifetime. She experimentally arched her back. That helped a bit. She stretched one arm, one leg at a time. She almost cried with frustration. It was useless. With her muscles cramped and screaming she would be no match for them when they finally opened the trunk. Still she had to try. She could at least yell bloody murder.

The car came to a halt. Caitlin positioned herself so her feet were against the trunk lid. If she could get in a good kick as they extracted her, while at the same time screaming her lungs out…

The trunk lid came up, the light temporarily blinding her. She kicked out with both feet, connecting with flesh and hearing a satisfying grunt. She opened her mouth to scream, only to have it stuffed with a foul smelling rag. The dirty blanket was once again wrapped around her thrashing kicking figure.

"Take her feet, I've got her shoulders. *Vite, vite,* before somebody sees."

Caitlin was hauled unceremoniously out of the trunk and thrown across someone's shoulders. Blinded by the blanket, head bobbing down, she was aware of them entering a building and ascending stairs that wound round and round, her body bumping against the walls as they ascended. She counted twenty, twenty eight. Probably a house, then, not a warehouse like Allen. At the thought of Allen, nausea almost overtook her.

She was thrown down. The surface wasn't hard. A bed? No one said a word, but footsteps receded and a door closed and she sensed she was alone. She wriggled out of the disgusting blanket and pulled the gag out of her mouth. Ugh! She tried to spit but couldn't summon the saliva.

Where was she? It looked like a small attic bedroom. Saints be praised, there was a toilet and washbasin. She made use of the facilities and then filled her mouth with water again and again. She had no idea whether the water was safe to drink, but she cupped her hands and drank her fill. Unsafe water was the least of her worries at this point. On a towel bar beside the sink was a tattered towel. It had seen better days but was immaculately clean. She used it to wash off as much of the dirt from the filthy car trunk as she could.

Once these simple needs were taken care of, she was more herself. She took a good look around the room. An attic room, all dormer shaped. Small and whitewashed. Clean. The bed was covered with a clean white sheet. A small table stood beside it. There was a simple rush-seated wooden chair in the corner, but no other furnishings. The door looked heavy, stout carved oak. Experimentally, Caitlin turned the knob. Locked, of course. There were narrow windows in the dormers, too high to see out. Caitlin pulled the chair over to one and stood on it. Standing on tiptoe, she could see rain glistening on a cobblestone street below. And across the street? She could scarcely believe her eyes. There was what appeared to be a walled medieval town on an island, connected to the mainland only by a narrow bridge. She could see a high stone gate surmounted by a clock tower. A black and white flag flew over the ramparts. Between the walled town and the cobbled stone street on which her captor's house sat, small fishing boats were pulled haphazardly up on a stony beach. Waves lapped the shore. There were fishing nets strung out around and between the boats. Blue nets. She'd never seen blue fishing nets before. Where could she be? It had seemed like a lifetime when she was in the trunk of that car, but her watch had survived the encounter. It was only a little over four hours since they'd drugged her and thrown her into the trunk. Not enough time to get to the South Coast. It had to be the Atlantic coast, Normandy or Brittany.

She got down from her perch and went over to sit on the cot. What was this place? This is not what she would have expected of a hide-away for either Nic Bisset or Jules Allard. It reminded her of some of the simpler hostel rooms she'd stayed in on a trip in her student days. Basic, simple, but clean and comfortable.

What were Colin and Aristotle doing at this moment? When they realized she was missing, they would have gone to the police, of course. But they would have no idea where she was.

There was a sound at the door. A key rattled and turned in the latch and the door swung open to reveal Jules standing there, gun ominously pointed. He stepped in, followed by a silent woman with a tray.

The woman, dressed all in black, with long voluminous skirts covered by a huge white apron, set the tray with bread and cheese and a small carafe of wine on the bedside table.

"*Bonjour, Madam.*" Caitlin rushed into speech. "*Au secour!* Help me. I'm being held prisoner." Caitlin took the woman by the arm. "Help me please! Call the police."

Jules laughed. "*Tante* Louise is both deaf and

dumb and she does what I tell her to do."

The woman backed out of the room without ever raising her eyes to Caitlin's. As she left, Nic entered and stood, back to the door.

Jules came over and perched backways on the chair with his arm stretched along the top. He had changed his bloody shirt for a clean one. It appeared Caitlin hadn't broken his nose, as had been her intention.

His voice was all the more deadly because it was mild and conversational. "I'd like to give you a taste of what you gave me in Paris, but we'll leave you unharmed for the moment. Just do as you're told and you may survive. But give us grief and I'll turn you over to Nic and his knife. I personally don't care whether you live or die, but you're worth more to us alive than dead, so it's to my advantage to keep Nic away from you." He shrugged a very Gallic shrug. "You may get out of this with your life if you do exactly as instructed."

"What do you want of me?"

The suddenness of the backhanded slap across the face stunned Caitlin and brought tears to her eyes.

"Don't treat me like a fool. You know the whereabouts of the dragon. And we mean to have it. We spent five years in prison for that theft. The dragon is ours by rights."

"Nic?" Jules turned to his colleague. "Search her."

In three strides, Nic was across the room. Caitlin screamed as he grabbed her shirt in one hand and with his knife in the other sliced it from neckline to hem. He looked at her fragile lace bra. "No hiding place there." He gave what might have been in anyone else a laugh.

Then he pulled her jeans off. He paused for a

moment, his gaze traveling over her nearly nude body, enjoying her discomfort. He turned the pants pockets out perfunctorily, finding only a few euros and her cell phone. These he threw down in disgust. "Nothing here. She doesn't have it on her."

"No. It was too much to hope she would," Jules said. "But we have her, and they're going to want her back. The girl for the dragon. Not a bad exchange."

He nodded toward the doorway and they both went over to the door. There Jules turned back. "We'll give your two boyfriends a few hours to worry. Then we'll set up the exchange. A live girl for an amulet. I think they'll be reasonable. Especially if you can supply a realistic scream of terror in the background when I call. Nic can help out there. He has a talent with the knife."

Caitlin heard the door slam and the turning of the key in the lock. She raised her hand to her face where Jules had slapped her. It still stung.

Picking up the remnants of her clothes, she shook her head. Not wearable. She wrapped the bed sheet around her for warmth.

Then she looked at the tray on the table. She'd better eat the bread and cheese. Who knew when the next meal might be? But she'd give the wine a pass. It could be drugged, and she needed to keep her wits about her.

She shivered. The room was cold. Pulling the sheet more closely around her, she eyed the filthy blanket and decided she'd rather be cold. If only she'd taken her jacket with her this morning instead of just slipping some money and her phone in her pocket.

Her phone! They hadn't taken it from her. It was where Nic had thrown it down. On the floor. Was it charged? She couldn't remember.

She still had some battery. Praise be the saints. She'd text. That would be better than attempting a call. What could she tell them? Quickly she typed in,

—Coast. Walled town, blue fishing nets, black and white flag, attic. Hurry!—

Her battery died on the last words. Had the message gone through? Had it been enough? Would they find her before Nic tried his knife on her? She shivered again, this time not from the cold.

Chapter Ten

Colin and André were sitting in the bar of the Amiral in Concarneau when Aristotle walked in.

"Thank God you're here." Colin grasped Aristotle's hand. "Thanks to you we know she's in Brittany, but we don't know where to begin."

André spoke to the black man who was Colin's friend. "It was clever of you to follow them and to get their license plate. It should simplify our job."

"It should have made it easy, but it didn't. Even with the license number and location, the police couldn't find the car and stop it. Why was that?" Aristotle looked at André with something bordering on accusation. "I know you and Colin are old friends, but the police haven't been much help so far. I'm not quite certain why you are here or what you think you can do to help."

André took a deep breath. "I was involved in the police operation six years ago, when one of my fellow officers was wounded and Alain Tremont walked out of the Louvre with a priceless gem in his hands. It happened on my watch. And I'm as certain as I can be of anything, somebody in the Louvre was in league with Tremont. In league with all three of the thieves. I need to find out who that person was."

"Right now I'm much more concerned about finding Caitlin than about a crime that happened six years ago." Aristotle cursed under his breath. "I shouldn't have lost them. It was sheer carelessness on my part."

"On the contrary, you did a great job of following them," André said. "There were only three choices they could have made at that roundabout. One small inland town, or Pont-Aven at the mouth of the river, or Concarneau. They'll be in one of those towns—and the most likely bet is right here in Concarneau. Jules' roots are here. He still has family here. I had reason to meet with them after the affair at the Louvre. They're good, seafaring people for the most part, not very proud of their connection with a jewel thief, but they will protect their own. Jules will find help here and he knows his way around these parts. This is where we'll find him."

Colin's phone vibrated, signaling a message. His hand was shaking as he read Caitlin's words to the others. "She's in Concarneau. She can see the old walled island town and the black and white Breton flag and boats with blue fishing nets on the beach. She has to be near us."

He stood and headed for the door of the Amiral. "There it is, right in front of us. She's somewhere very close. Somewhere in that row of houses." He scanned the houses facing the harbor and the old walled town. "Let's go. We need to search the area, house by house if necessary."

"Wait a minute. You can't just go off, halfcocked, asking questions." André put his hand on Colin's arm. "We'll need authority from the local police to do a house by house search. I'll check in with the *Commissariat de Police*. It's just a couple of blocks from here. Wait for me. I shouldn't be long."

Aristotle called after him, "Ask them if any of the houses close by belong to the Allard family. That could shorten our search considerably."

****

Caitlin moved through a series of exercises, stretching her arms and legs, running in place, arching her back. Her muscles ached from the three hours of confinement in the trunk of the car. She had to be ready to move when she had a chance. Finally, chilled and exhausted, she lay down on the narrow cot and pulled the white sheet tightly around her. With nothing more to do, she could only wait and hope Colin had received her message and might be able to deduce from it where she was.

She must have dozed, because she became aware of a gentle hand on her shoulder, shaking her awake. She opened her eyes to see a face hovering over her. The woman who had brought her bread and cheese, *Tante* Louise. She pulled at Caitlin, indicating the open door.

Caitlin shook her head to clear it. The woman was helping her escape? She jumped off the bed and gave her an impulsive hug. "Thank you, thank you!"

The woman put her finger to her lips indicating the need for stealth. Together they crossed the room and slipped out the door. The woman closed the door behind them and turned the key in the lock. On tiptoe, they descended one flight. Caitlin heard steps ascending. Male voices, Jules and Nic. She motioned frantically to *Tante* Louise.

Understanding at once, *Tante* Louise pulled her through a door into a room much like the one she'd just left, except it had higher ceilings and was more comfortably furnished. They waited just inside the door as the steps went past and up to the room they'd just vacated.

Tante Louise crossed the room and opened the window. She pushed Caitlin toward it, indicating she should climb out onto a small patch of slate roof.

There were shouts from the upstairs room and footsteps hammering down the stairs.

Caitlin looked with apprehension at the slippery slate, but did as instructed. The window closed behind her. When she glanced back into the room, *Tante* Louise was sitting in a rocking chair, knitting. Caitlin pulled herself over to a chimney post and, hiding behind it, held on tight. It was beginning to drizzle and within minutes she was soaked, shivering uncontrollably, as water ran in rivulets down her nearly nude body. She could hear Nic and Jules shouting at *Tante* Louise and she could imagine the placid woman, unable to hear or respond to their curses, simply continuing her knitting.

Then she heard their voices below her, on the street. "She can't have gone far. She's on foot and she knows no one here. You go along the harbor and I'll search the street and parked cars. Look in the boats on the beach. She may have taken shelter in one of them." Their voices receded as they moved off on their search.

The window open and *Tante* Louise motioned her back in.

Caitlin couldn't stop shaking. She saw a dark red streak across the other woman's face. One of the men had stuck her.

Tante Louise went into a small adjoining room and returned with a towel and a soft clean blanket. She motioned for Caitlin to remove her wet underclothes. Within moments Caitlin stood sheathed only in a blanket.

Meanwhile, Tante Louise was rummaging in an old chest. Men's underwear. Baggy cotton knit drawers and matching undershirt. Trousers. Not slacks, men's trousers. Black with a button fly. A button fly? How old must those be? But they fit. A white shirt, full sleeved with a vest to go over. And a warm black woolen jacket.

In spite of her precarious situation, Caitlin laughed. They were looking for a woman and she was going to be a man. Tante Louise stood back to admire her handiwork. She shook her head and pushed Caitlin down in the chair. She pulled her hair up tightly and braided it, a process more than a little uncomfortable. Then she took out of the chest a wide brimmed black hat of the kind Breton men wore on special occasions and anchored it over Caitlin's hair.

She motioned for Caitlin to stand and she walked a circle around her. She looked toward Caitlin's feet and shook her head. Caitlin understood. The running shoes would have to go. They were soaked through anyway. A few moments later she had on warm woolen socks and black boots just little too big. Better than too small, Caitlin thought.

The woman reached once more into her treasure chest and came up with a card identifying the bearer as one Jean Pitou. The picture could have been anyone, Caitlin thought. Even her. This should give her some time to make an effective escape.

Impulsively, she leaned over and kissed the other woman on the cheek. *Tante* Louise blushed beet red and pushed Caitlin toward the door. Caitlin eased it open and listened. Silence. She turned to make her goodbyes to the woman who was helping her, only to have wad of euros and a large black umbrella thrust into her hands. The woman made the sign of the cross as if to say, "Go with God."

Caitlin vowed if she ever got out of this mess, she would return to thank *Tante* Louise properly. She ran down the remaining flight of steps and opened the door a crack. No one in sight. She slid out, closing the door behind her and hurried along the cobblestone street with the umbrella open, keeping close to the buildings, in the shadows as much as possible. Nic emerged from behind one of the boats on the beach and for a moment she froze in panic. Then she forced herself to walk on. He hadn't even noticed her. She was a local. She was a man.

She must have been walking for about twenty minutes, away from the sea front, away from where the two men were searching for her, when she saw a bus pulled up at a marked bus stop. Number 47. Where was it going? It didn't matter as long as it was away from here. She boarded and offered the driver a twenty-euro note. He shook his head and pointed to the machine at the bus stop where she must buy a ticket. Reluctantly, she went back to the machine, keeping one eye on the bus; it mustn't leave without her. She managed on the third try to get a ticket for Pont-Aven, wherever that was.

Seated in the warm dry bus, bouncing along a narrow, winding, rough road, she saw a roadside sign with the name of the town and a slash across it indicating they were leaving Concarneau. She'd been in

Concarneau? Would Colin have recognized the town from her brief description? If he had even received her message. Could he and Aristotle be in Concarneau even now, searching for her?

As soon as possible, she would have to phone them to tell them where she was. Aristotle must be frantic, and Colin—she didn't even want to contemplate Colin's reaction to her disappearance.

She settled back in the deep seat, able to breathe again. She had done it. She'd escaped. She'd be in touch with Colin and Aristotle as soon as she could. Meanwhile she'd try to work her way back to Paris. Circuitously. No direct trains. Nic and Jules might well be looking for her on those. She had no desire to end up in their hands again.

It was an hour later when the bus pulled over and stopped. The other people on the bus all filed to get out. End of the line, Caitlin thought. She followed the crowd.

She helped a woman who was struggling to get off the bus with an infant in arms and a three year old and a number of packages.

"*Merci beaucoup.*" The woman smiled at Caitlin.

Caitlin risked a question, lowering her voice to match her male persona. "Where are we?" she ventured in her high school French.

"*C'est Pont-Aven,*" the woman replied.

"You wouldn't perhaps have a telephone I could use?"

"*Je regret...non. Peut-être à l'hôtel?*"

"*Merci.*" Of course. It was evening. She'd need something to eat and someplace to sleep. And a hotel would have telephones.

She glanced around to get her bearings and did a double take. Where had she landed? Pont-Aven looked like a set for Brigadoon. Narrow cobblestone streets wound in unexpected directions, lined with quaint higgledy-piggledy stone houses. It was a small town, steep and hilly, stretching along a riverbank bordered with rhododendrons and weeping willows. Where she had descended from the bus, the river was hardly more than a stream, but to her right it widened out enough to harbor a number of sailboats and other small pleasure craft.

Fear gripped her, making her stomach clench. She shivered, looking over her shoulder. She needed to get out of sight. Turning her back to the river, she headed up one of the steep, narrow streets. Every house had some kind of shop on the ground floor. Not the kind of shops aimed at the local population. These looked like glitzy tourist shops and, and…art galleries? Numerous shops had paintings in their windows. Here in the middle of nowhere. Where had she landed? She was Dorothy transported to Oz. No refuge here.

At the top of the hill she spotted a three-story white building. A hotel? Heading toward it, she sighed with relief when she saw a wrought-iron sign saying "pension" hanging in front.

Would her fake ID be enough to get her a room for the night? She looked over her shoulder apprehensively. She had to get off the streets. She was too vulnerable here by far. And she had to let Colin and Aristotle know where she was.

She squared her shoulders and, screwing up her courage, she marched into the inn.

No one was there. The small lobby was empty, the

front desk was unattended. Her breath came out in a whoosh. She wasn't sure what she expected, but not this.

Pulling herself together, she looked around. This was an inn, there must be an innkeeper somewhere. She spied a bell on the counter and banged her hand on it.

An old man ambled out of an adjoining room. He glowered at her over the top of bifocals.

"*Vous voudrais?*"

"*Une chambre pour la nuit, s'il vous plait.*" Caitlin grumbled out the words, putting her ID on the counter between them.

The innkeeper barely glanced at the identity card. "*Cent-vingt-trois euros.*"

Caitlin almost panicked. How much was that? She shoved two hundred euros across the counter, and was relieved when he took it and gave her back a pile of bills and coins.

"*Numéro douze au deuxième étage.*" He shoved a key across the desk. He had turned to shamble back into his inner sanctum before Caitlin could ask about a telephone. She hoped there would be one in the room.

She looked at the miniscule, claustrophobic lift and opted instead to climb the three flights of stairs to what in France was called the second floor. Number twelve was the last room on the left.

A double bed, a bedside table, a chair. A chest of drawers with a small mirror over it. It was much like the room she had been in before she escaped. The bed linens were nicer and there was a window with pretty fabric drapes. And there was a small bathroom with a high sided tub. What there wasn't, was a telephone.

Caitlin glanced in the mirror. Her hair had come

loose and was tumbling around her shoulders, giving her a decidedly feminine appearance. So much for her disguise. Should she just comb it out or should she stick it back under the hat? She was going to have to go back downstairs and ask to use a telephone. Trying to resume her male identity was rather like locking the barn door after the horse was stolen, but it made her feel somehow safer. She took a few minutes to effect the necessary repairs and headed back down to the lobby.

The innkeeper was in the back room, speaking with someone on the telephone. Good. They had a telephone. She didn't mean to eavesdrop but she couldn't help herself. The old man must be hard of hearing. He was almost shouting into the phone.

"This is Gerard Germain. I heard from Père Allard you were seeking a package?"

Caitlin backed up so she wouldn't be in the old man's sight line. Père Allard? It couldn't be—

Then she heard him say, "And the finder's fee would be…? *Bien. La Pension Beaupont à Pont-Aven.* Room twelve on the second floor."

Caitlin was dizzy with shock. Their influence reached this far? How widely had they put out a "watch for" warning? And where could she find refuge in this small town where she knew no one?

She glanced at the reception desk. The pension had only twelve rooms. Would they search them all if they didn't find her in room twelve? Perhaps. But they might just think she had been scared off and taken shelter elsewhere. Keeping the key to room twelve she slipped around the desk and removed a key for a room on the ground floor. She hoped no one would observe its absence. There was still one key hanging on the slot.

And she might have a better chance of getting away from them if she had a room nearer to an outside door.

The old man came out just as she reached the proper side of the desk again.

"May I use your telephone, please?"

"*Ce n'est pas possible.*"

"But if course it's possible," Caitlin persisted. "You have a telephone. I pay you. I use the telephone."

"*Ce n'est pas possible.*" The old man shambled back into his office and shut the door firmly.

What now? Where were Colin and Aristotle? How long would it take them to get here? She had to get to a telephone. Maybe she had fifteen minutes before she ran to ground. Perhaps a café?

She headed at a jogging pace toward one of the streets she had noted earlier, one that appeared to exist for the tourist trade. There was a café halfway down the block.

She sat inside, out of sight, rather than at one of the outside tables. When the middle-aged, motherly-looking waitress came, she ordered a coffee, and as an afterthought a *croque-monsieur*, that meal on bread the French eat when in a hurry. Danger made her hungry.

The server disappeared into the kitchen and a few minutes later brought her sandwich. Caitlin glanced at her watch. How much time did she have?

In her husky approximation of a male voice she asked, "Do you have a telephone I could use?" she asked. "I'll pay the charges."

The woman raised her brows in curiosity, but said, "*Mais oui*, no problem." She fished a mobile out of her pocket.

Caitlin took the proffered phone with shaking

hands and slumped back against her chair, her whole body released from tension she hadn't even fully realized she'd had. She was light-headed with relief.

Colin answered on the first ring. On hearing Caitlin's voice, he shouted, "Where are you?"

"In Pont-Aven, in a café. I checked in at the Pension Beaupont. But they know I'm here. They're on their way now."

"We're already moving. André will alert the police there. Can you stay some place safe, out of sight until we get there?"

"I took a key to a different room. Number one on the ground floor. They think I'm on the second floor, room number twelve."

"Good. Stay in the room until we arrive. We're on our way!"

As the connection was severed, she was full of doubts. Should she return to the hotel? That's where Jules and Nic were headed. Where they expected to find her in Room 12 on the second floor. They could intercept her even before she got to the room on the ground floor for which she had pilfered the key. And if they didn't, it wouldn't take them long to discover her ruse, to search the hotel, and find her. Her clever idea didn't seem quite so clever on second thought. They might well arrive well before Colin and Aristotle. And she had no great faith the police would arrive in time. Nic and Jules could have her in the trunk of a car again in two shakes. She shivered. She couldn't let that happen. Where could she find refuge, if not in the hotel?

Chapter Eleven

The waitress approached with her bill. Caitlin took off her hat and shook out her hair.

The woman stopped in her tracks. "*Vous êtes femme!*"

"*Oui. Parlez-vous Anglais?*" Do you speak English?

"A little."

"Yes, I'm a woman and I'm in grave trouble. There are two seriously dangerous men on my trail. I need a safe place to hide."

"You run from the police? From an abusive husband?"

"From two criminals who are threatening my life. I promise you I've done nothing wrong." *If you don't count concealing a national treasure.*

The woman studied her for a moment, then her lips relaxed and she nodded sharply. "Upstairs. *Mon appartemente.* Just for a short time."

Caitlin was close to tears with relief. "That would be wonderful. Thank you. With any luck, my"—what could she call Colin and Aristotle—"my friends will be here soon to help me."

"We should call the police, I think."

"I believe my friends have already done so."

"*Bien.* Hurry. *Vite, vite.* You will be safe here for a little while." She led Caitlin through the kitchen, up a

138

steep set of stairs.

As Caitlin followed her to the apartment, she realized she would be well and truly trapped if this helpful-seeming woman was one of Jules Allard's relatives. But no. Even Jules couldn't be related to everybody in Brittany.

The woman held out her hand. "I'm Juliette Arnot."

"And I'm Caitlin Abernathy. *Merci beaucoup* for your help."

"To tell zee truth, it is, how you say, fun. You can't imagine how dull Pont-Aven can be once *les touristes* depart." The woman went to her armoire and pulled out a heavy sweater and a pair of jeans and, laughing, held them against herself. They were clearly several sizes too small. She pretended to spoon food into her mouth and mimed her hips getting wider and wider. "*J'adore la cuisine!*"

Caitlin burst out laughing for the first time since she had been abducted.

Juliette handed the clothes to Caitlin and mimed that she should remove the ones she was wearing.

"*Merci beaucup*, thank you," Caitlin said as she took off her clothes, stepped into Juliette's jeans and pulled the cable knit sweater over her head. They were a perfect fit.

She folded the wool suit and white shirt carefully and placing the wide brimmed hat on top, handed them to Juliette.

"*S'il vous plait*, please, save the clothes I'm wearing. I'd like to return them to the kind woman, *une femme gentille*, in Concarneau who lent them to me. I think they may have once belonged to someone she cared for, *son cher ami*." Caitlin placed her hands over her heart.

"*Entendu*." Juliette nodded her understanding. "*Mais vos cheveux,*" she ran her fingers through Caitlin's hair, "you try to hide, you must do something with the hair." She went to her bureau. "*Voila!*" She tied a scarf around Caitlin's hair, gypsy style, obscuring it almost entirely.

"I hope my friends will arrive soon. They'll be all the protection I need."

"And how will I know them? I would not like to lead the wrong people to you."

"You can't miss them. Aristotle is very tall and very black with hair almost down to his waist."

"*Mon dieu!*"

"And Colin is almost as tall and has red hair and a beard."

"You have unusual friends."

"They aren't just my friends, they're the only family I have, and I love them." Caitlin listened to what she'd just said so impulsively. She did love them both. Aristotle was the big brother she'd never had, and Colin...

"I must get back to the café. My evening customers, my regulars, arrive soon. "

"Could I use your phone once more? I need to tell Colin where I am."

Juliette handed her phone to Caitlin.

When Caitlin punched in the number there was only static. They must be in a dead spot on the way here. What should she do? They expected her to be in the hotel. But she just couldn't return to possible capture by those two sadistic bastards.

"You can try to call your friends again in a few minutes." Juliette indicated a table with an old-fashioned telephone on it as she headed for the stairs.

****

Colin was shouting in Gaelic. Aristotle had never heard the words before but he recognized them as serious swearing. If he ever used bad language, he too would be swearing. The three of them stood on the grassy bank, looking at the tire, flat as a pancake. The boot of the car was open. No spare tire. They were in a dead spot, unable either to use their cell phones to call for help, or to warn Caitlin of their delay.

André shook his head. "It's my fault. I changed the tire and left my spare to be repaired. I was supposed to pick it up this morning."

"What do we do now?" Colin sounded frantic.

"How far is it?" Aristotle asked André.

"A couple of kilometers."

"Run!" Aristotle said. "Maybe we'll get cell reception somewhere along the way."

Andre said, "I'll stay with the car. Send help."

Aristotle was off running before André finished talking, Colin only a few steps behind him.

Fifteen minutes later the two were on the outskirts of the town. Aristotle paused to catch his breath. "The Pension Beaupont?" he yelled at a woman pushing a baby carriage across the street.

She looked at him and rushed on without answering, glancing back at him in fear.

Colin paused and wiped the sweat off his face with his sleeve. "No offense, mate. She's probably never seen anything like the two of us in her life."

"This one looks more likely." Colin approached a

man coming down the road with a fishing pole. "*Pardon, monsieur*, could you direct us to the Pension Beaupont?"

The man hesitated, looking the two of them up and down, then without a word, gestured to a road leading off to the left.

"You get a feeling the natives aren't very friendly?" Aristotle asked.

"We don't exactly look like tourists," Colin answered, trotting up the road the man had indicated, Aristotle at his heels.

In front of the pension, the two stopped. "What now?" Aristotle said. "Do we just storm in?"

"Let's try asking politely."

In the small reception hall, Colin banged the bell on the desk.

There was no response. "Room one on this floor." They charged down the hall and Colin flung the door open. No Caitlin. The room was unused. There was no sign anyone had been there.

"Upstairs, room twelve." They headed up the stairs, Aristotle motioning Colin to quiet his footsteps. Stopping at the entrance to the second floor, they peered cautiously around the corner.

The door to room twelve was open and a small elderly man was standing in it, saying, "But she was here, Jules, I tell you. An hour ago. She'd just checked in when I called you!"

Jules Allard pushed past him, snarling, "Well, she's not here now, so where is she?"

"She wanted to use the telephone and I didn't let her. Maybe she went out to find one."

Colin hurried back down the stairs, motioning for

Aristotle to follow him. At the first floor landing, they ducked into the hallway as Jules hurried past.

"What now?" Aristotle whispered.

"She said she was calling from a café. We need to check out any cafés close to here."

"Allard will be doing the same thing. Looking for anyplace Caitlin could have found a phone."

Colin ran quickly down the stairs followed by Aristotle, and paused at the entrance to the pension. "We follow him."

"We're not exactly inconspicuous. How do you propose we do that?

Colin was already heading out the door. "We split up. You follow at a distance. Just keep me in sight. He's going to connect up with Nic at some point. If they go separate ways you take Nic, I'll take Jules.

****

Caitlin paced back and forth in the small apartment. She hadn't been able to reach Colin or Aristotle. Where were they? Why didn't they answer their phones? They must be at the *pension* by now, expecting to find her there. Should she return to the Pension Beaupont? They said were going to call the police. It should be safe by now.

Still she hesitated. Somehow she knew she was safer here. She picked up the phone and tried again. She almost cried with relief when Colin answered.

"Where are you?"

He sounded out of breath, as if he'd been running.

"A café. I don't know the name, but it's close to the hotel. Where are you?"

"Almost there. Stay out of sight!"

When she heard footsteps on the stairs, Caitlin

rushed to the door and opened it.

Nic Bisset smirked and said, "Bonjour Mademoiselle," as he drove the needle into her arm.

****

Colin and Aristotle paused at the entrance to the café.

Jules Allard was deep in conversation with the waitress. "I haven't any idea what you're talking about," she was saying. "There's been no one of that description here. " She nodded to the tables, now nearly all filled. "Just my regulars. And I'm busy now, as you can see. So if you don't want anything else—"

Jules grabbed her arm and twisted it behind her back. "Where is she?"

Juliette screamed in pain, and chairs screeched on the floor or overturned as patrons jumped to their feet.

"Let go of the lady!" Colin shouted.

Jules found himself airborne and then on the floor with Colin standing menacingly over him. Some men in the crowd moved forward.

With the slipperiness of an eel, Jules ducked through Colin's legs, grabbed a chair and brought it down on Colin's head, leaving him swaying dizzily.

Aristotle weighed into the fray as patrons screamed, some trying to get through the crowded doorway, others joining in the fight.

Juliette ran behind the bar and ducked down, taking out her cell phone to call the police.

Moments later the police arrived to find a full brawl in process, chairs and china flying through the air. They plowed into the fray, whistles blowing. The locals, recognizing authority, stepped back, leaving two very un-French looking characters alone in the middle of the room.

Colin was dazed, blood trickling down his face from a scalp wound. He had the promise of what was going to be a very black eye. Aristotle hadn't fared much better. His neat ponytail had come undone and dreadlocks covered much of his face. His vest was torn and he swayed uncertainly.

Before they knew what was happening they were both in handcuffs.

"Caitlin—" Colin managed.

Juliette came out from behind the protection of the bar. "You're the two she's been expecting. She's upstairs. I'll go get her."

"What?" the policeman said, as he hustled the two strangers to toward the door.

"*Un moment*," Juliette said. "I'm sure everything will explain itself in one moment. Let me get Caitlin."

She disappeared up the steps to her apartment. They heard her steps clattering back down a moment latter. "She's not there. She's gone!"

"Son of a bitch," Colin yelled. "They've got her! They must have slipped her out during the fight."

Aristotle shook his head, trying to clear his fuddled brain. "Maybe she just ran away. She might have been frightened."

"No. Look. They're both missing. Allard and Bisset. They're both gone. Goddammit!" Colin struggled against the handcuffs. He turned to the police. "Please. You've got the wrong men. You've got to find Nic Bisset and Jules Allard. They've got a record as long as your arm. And they've kidnapped Caitlin again. You've got to act now or they'll get away."

"Kidnapped?" the first officer paused for a

moment.

Juliette chimed in, "Please, Henri." She put her arm on the arm of the larger of the two gendarmes. "Listen to them. A young woman, Caitlin her name was, she was hiding upstairs, in fear for her life."

The policeman looked down at his friend. "Perhaps, but I haven't the authority, Juliette. The *Police Judiciaire* will have to decide what's to be done." The two policemen pushed Colin and Aristotle out the door and hustled them into the waiting police car.

****

Colin and Aristotle were in a small cell together, chafing over the lost time. Someone had come in to attend to their cuts and bruises, but when they asked to see the "judge," they were told he had been sent for. He had to come from Concarneau.

It seemed like hours before they were led to an office and invited to sit down and explain themselves to a middle-aged man who looked more like a shopkeeper than a judge.

The judge looked over his glasses at them. "Who are you and what are you doing in Pont Aven? Besides breaking up one of our better cafés, that is?"

Colin pushed his EU passport and Aristotle his American one across the desk in response and related the events so far. "We found Allard and Bisset here in Pont Aven, but they got away again during the fight. And they've got Caitlin with them. Please, do something!"

"A stolen motorcycle?"

Colin shouted. "You're missing the point here! A woman has been taken hostage and is being held against her will!"

The judge pushed a button on his intercom. "Check on a motorcycle stolen yesterday on the rue de Lille."

Juliette burst in. The young policeman following her said, "I'm sorry, sir. She just rushed past the front desk. Shall I remove her?"

The judge peered at her. "Do you know anything about this?"

"She was in my apartment. She was terrified. She'd escaped from them, but she was afraid they would find her before these two got here. And it seems they did. And now my cafe is a shambles and who, I ask, is going to pay for the damages? That's what I get for trying to be helpful."

"Sorry about that," Colin said. "I'll pay for the damages, but Caitlin—"

The door opened again and André Bergère strolled in. With a warning glance at Colin and Aristotle, he addressed the judge. "Good afternoon, Maurice. I see you've met my friends."

"Bergère. I might have known you had a hand in this. Don't tell me. It's something that could have international repercussions."

André coughed but didn't answer.

"I see. If I release these two in your custody, can I have your assurance they won't cause any further property damage?"

"Absolutely, sir."

The judge sighed.

Colin interjected, "Please. You must put out an alert for Jules Allard and Nic Bisset."

"Hmm. I know Allard did time for theft, but he has a number of relatives and friends around here. I'll do what I can, but he may not be easy to find."

André spoke. "He has abducted a young woman, sir. An American."

The judge raised his eyebrows. "An American? Yes, that could be a problem. Very well. I'll see the police in the area are alerted."

****

Caitlin regained consciousness, sick in her stomach, and with a pounding headache. She was lying on the floor. A very dirty, dusty floor. She adjusted her position and discovered her right hand was fastened by a handcuff to the pipe of an old-fashioned iron radiator. Her feet were bound as well. They were leaving nothing to chance this time.

By careful maneuvering, she was able to sit up and take stock of her surroundings. She was in a large space. Not the kind anyone lived in. Pallid light came through a dirty window. A warehouse? Allen had been murdered in a warehouse. She shivered, but not from the cold.

Footsteps. The door opened.

Her two captors crossed the open space and stared down at her with cold eyes. She tried unsuccessfully to repress the tremor coursing through her.

"Where is it? Where's the amulet?" Nic's voice was quiet and deadly.

"I don't know. I don't know what you're talking about," Caitlin mumbled.

Jules spoke softly, the voice of reason. "Just tell us where it is and you'll be free to go. You can have a little time to think about it, but I hope you'll find the right answers, because my friend Nic, here, is an artist with a knife. He knows how to peel a layer of skin off a girl like the peel off an orange. He'll start with your breasts. Have you any idea how painful that will be?"

Caitlin shuddered, but remained silent.

"Give her a little taste, Nic. Just a bit off her arm. We'll let her imagination do the rest."

Nic smiled and grabbed her arm. Before she had time to realize what was happening he had sliced off a strip of skin.

She gave a blood-curdling scream as the pain hit, intense and burning. She fought to keep the room from spinning, to deny them the pleasure of making her faint. Blood dribbled down her arm.

"We want to help you," Jules said. "You know what you have to do if you want to live." He grabbed a handful of her hair and wrenched her head back so she had to meet his expressionless, cold eyes. "I hope you'll find the right answers by the time we come back, because my friend Nic, here, would enjoy nothing more than carving you up like a chicken. What you just experienced is nothing to what he can do."

They left her slumped over, bruised and battered, blood snaking down her arm, in the dirty, deserted warehouse. Caitlin attempted to rouse herself, but she was immobile with shock. They were not going to let her live. Even if Colin and Aristotle gave them the amulet, they would not let her live, any more than they let Allen/Alain live. Neither Colin nor Aristotle would be safe. Nic and Jules had murdered once. They had nothing to lose by murdering again.

Chapter Twelve

André stayed behind, chatting with the judge as Colin and Aristotle consulted with the policeman who was Juliette's friend.

"How can I help?" The young police officer seemed anxious to make up for his earlier treatment of the two men.

Colin said, "We need all the addresses of properties owned by members of the Allard family in Brittany. Can you help us with that? Quickly?"

"Yes, of course. I can access that information on my computer."

"It's a place to start," Aristotle said. "Begin with Concarneau. I'm pretty sure those two won't have stayed around Pont Aven once they had Caitlin."

The officer left them with the open file. It was many pages long. They had to wade through all the A's in each district to find the Allards.

André came into the room sometime later. "How's it going?"

With bloodshot eyes, Colin looked at André. "There are a few possibilities."

Aristotle grunted. "What we've found is there are a hell of a lot of Allards in Brittany."

André sighed. "And there's nothing to say Nic and Jules stayed around here. They could already have taken her back to Paris for all we know. Perhaps we should return there and leave this in the hands of the police."

"I don't think so!" Aristotle looked up, bleary eyed, from the computer screen. "The police haven't been much help so far. I'm not about to trust Caitlin's life to them at this point."

"We have to begin somewhere, André. We can't just wait for them to contact us. What if they—?" Colin couldn't put the possibility of harm coming to Caitlin into words. It was unthinkable. "We have to try. Let's look at the closest ones. The ones in Concarneau."

"Well, so far I've come up with a residence, a tobacco shop, and a crêperie in Concarneau," Aristotle said. "None of them look very promising as a place to stash somebody out of sight."

"They killed Alain, didn't they? What's to keep them from killing Caitlin?" Colin looked at the other two men, desperation in his eyes.

Aristotle put a hand on his shoulder. "They won't kill Caitlin yet, Colin. They need her to get the amulet. She's their bargaining chip."

"I hope you're right."

Colin's phone buzzed. "Colin Stryker here."

There was a pause and then a low laugh. "And Nic Bisset here. We have a package I think belongs to you. I'll put her on."

"Colinnn!" Caitlin's voice rose in a scream.

Colin's hands shook. "What are you doing to her? If you hurt her I swear I'll kill you if it's the last thing I do."

"She's not seriously damaged—yet. We just wanted to be sure we had your attention, Professor. Concarneau. The bridge to the old town, under the clock, at midnight. Our package for yours." The phone was disconnected.

The three sat in silence for a moment. It was André who spoke first. "That answers one question. They're in Concarneau. But I somehow doubt they'll have her with them at the bridge to the old town. Or even if we'll see them."

"What do you mean?" Colin's voice was hoarse with tension. "They said their package for ours."

André sighed. "This is what happens in kidnapping cases, Colin. We'll get another phone call when we get there at midnight. It will instruct us to leave the package there, or even someplace else, and leave. They'll say they'll tell us where she is after they've inspected the amulet and gotten away. In point of fact, they will never call again. They'll never tell us where she is. And they will not let her live. She can identify them in court."

"Oh, God! No!" Colin put is head in his hands.

Aristotle straightened his back. "We know now they're in Concarneau. But where in Concarneau?"

The young policeman came back into the room. "I don't know whether this will help," he said, "but I've marked the properties belonging to members of the Allard family in the immediate Concarneau area on a map for you." He spread it out on the table. "You can see, here's the old town, and the bridge." The four men hovered over the map. "I suggest you search close to there and widen out in a circle. I can call on the police in Concarneau for help if you wish me to."

André said, "If Allard and Bisset suspect police involvement—"

"You think Caitlin may be in increased danger if

they see uniformed police nosing around." Colin raised his head and looked hard at the young officer.

"Yes, it's possible. And you do have the help of Agent Bergère. A plainclothes policeman will arouse less suspicion."

"Right. Then it's up to us." Colin studied the map. "They won't kill her until they have the amulet. It's eight o'clock now. It means we have four hours to find her. You've marked three places near the old town."

"Yes." The officer pointed to the map. "See, the crêperie is here, and here is the tobacconist. And two streets over, right here, is a residence. They all belong to members of the Allard family."

"Thank you for your help." Colin stood and shook the young policeman's hand. "I'll keep you informed. We'd better get going."

Aristotle nodded. "We should split up. It will save time. Besides, one person is less intimidating than three. Colin, you try the crêperie. Order something and try asking casually about your old friend, Jules.

"André, take the private home. You can flash your badge if they're reticent. That leaves the tobacco shop for me. I'll claim to have known Allard in prison and see where it gets me."

"Do you think a photo of Caitlin might help?" Colin held out his phone and displayed a picture of Caitlin holding the piece of jewelry she had made for his mother. A shot Caitlin was not even aware he had taken. "I'll email it to each of you. I know it's a long shot, but—"

"It could come in handy," André agreed. "One hour, we meet at the Amiral. If we've uncovered nothing by then we will have to involve the Concarneau police."

****

André looked at the well-kept front garden and the prosperous looking stone house in front of him. Not the sort of environment he would have associated with Jules Allard. He rang the bell.

A middle-aged man, wearing a sweater and gray slacks, answered the door.

"Maurice Allard?"

The man nodded, "*Oui.*"

André showed his ID "I'd like to ask you a few questions if you have a moment."

The man looked puzzled, but stood aside and ushered André in.

André took out his iPhone. "Have you seen this young woman?"

The man studied the picture. "No." He paused and raised his voice. "Janine, come here. Have you seen this woman anyplace?"

A matronly looking woman came into the room, wiping her hands on her apron. She too studied the picture and shook her head. "No. Is she missing?"

"Yes. And we have reason to believe Jules Allard has abducted her and is holding her against her will."

The man's face became suffused with anger. "We have nothing to do with that man. I'm a schoolteacher and my wife is a nurse. Our name is respected in Concarneau. I might have known if the police came calling it would have something to do with that *fils de pute*! I'm afraid we can't help you. We have nothing to do with that side of the family."

André thanked the two for their cooperation and took his leave. He could report to the others he had interviewed his Allards, and they were not involved in Caitlin's disappearance. He knew that before he interviewed them. He wiped a smug smile off his face. Things were progressing just as he had hoped.

****

Colin entered the crêperie. It smelled of sugar and vanilla. His stomach rumbled. When had he last eaten? There were six delicate little wrought iron tables, with flimsy looking chairs. If he was going to engage anyone in conversation, he would have to order something.

A young woman wearing a traditional Breton dress and apron emerged from the kitchen and handed him a menu. On it were at least thirty varieties of crêpes.

Without studying it he said, "I'll have the *citron sucrée.*"

When she reappeared five minutes later with his order, he said, "I believe you may be related to an old friend of mine, Jules Allard. I'm trying to locate him."

The woman stepped back and stared at him. "Get out!" she hissed. "Now."

"Please," Colin said. "Just look at this picture. Have you seen her? We believe she may be with your cousin, Jules."

The woman said, "That man is no kin of ours, and, no, I haven't seen your woman. Now leave. And no. I don't want your money. Just get out!"

Colin left. What now?

****

At the tobacconist's Aristotle went to the rack of newspapers in the back of the shop. Picking up a copy of *Le Monde*, he approached the man behind the counter. He plunked a fifty-euro note down on the counter and said in fluent French, "I'm looking for an old friend, Jules Allard. I understand he comes from somewhere around here."

The man eyed the money. "Yes, I know Jules. He's my cousin. But if you are friends you should know where to find him."

"That's just it. He got out of jail three months ahead of me and we lost touch. I've got a job lined up I thought might interest him."

The man eyed the money again. "He was here a couple of days ago, but he left."

"Was anyone with him? A woman, perhaps?" Aristotle pulled out his phone and showed the shopkeeper Caitlin's picture.

The man barely glanced at it. "*Non. Il était seul.* He was alone." The shopkeeper pocketed the money.

Why did Aristotle not believe him? Was it the way he had avoided taking a good look at the photograph? Or was it the man's eyes, narrow slits, shifting around, avoiding ever looking directly at him?

Frustrated, he walked out of the shop, but lingered just outside the door, hoping the man might get on the phone to Allard, perhaps to warn him. But other customers came and went with nothing suspicious happening.

He was about to leave when someone tugged at his sleeve. A woman, looking around fearfully, was trying to pull him away from the tobacconist's shop, toward a small side street.

Checking to make sure no one was watching, he followed her. Out of sight of the shop, he said, "You've seen Caitlin? You know where she is?"

The woman nodded.

Aristotle let out a whoosh of relief. "Tell me where

156

she is. Her life is in danger."

The woman moved her hands in the language of the deaf.

She couldn't speak? Aristotle looked straight at her and spoke distinctly so she could read his lips. "I can't read your hands." He pulled out a small notebook and pencil and gave them to her. "Where is she?"

She shook her head and pulled him toward the street. She pointed.

There, across the harbor from the island of the old town, stood a row of dilapidated warehouses.

Before Aristotle could ask anything else of her, she was gone.

He pulled out his phone. "Reconvene now!"

****

Back at the Amiral, Aristotle told them what he had learned.

"There are at least a dozen warehouses in that row." Colin stood and headed for the door. "Come on. We've got to find Caitlin before those bastards harm her again." His hoarse voice reflected the strain he was under.

André put a restraining hand on his arm. "Sit down, Colin. Allard and Bisset won't be there. They think they have her safely stashed away. They have no motive to get rid of her until they have the amulet. And they won't be sitting in a cold, dusty warehouse in the meantime. They'll be someplace warm and comfortable, probably eating dinner."

"What are we waiting for?" Aristotle stood beside Colin. "Let's go."

"You can't mean to do this without the police," André said. "It would be breaking and entering. There are pretty strong laws about that. You don't want to end up in jail again. I'll go get help." He headed off at a trot in the direction of the local police station.

Aristotle looked after André's retreating form in astonishment. "Are we just going to stand here and wait for police help? That hasn't worked very well up to this point."

"No, we're not." Colin was already running, Aristotle close behind him. Down the road, around the end of the harbor, toward the row of buildings the deaf woman had pointed out to Aristotle.

Ten minutes later, they were there. There were even more buildings than they had thought when they looked across the water. Most were boarded up, their windows dirt-encrusted, their paint peeling and their roofs rusting. The whole area had an eerily deserted feeling, as if it had been forgotten by time.

"Let's separate, we can cover more territory more quickly that way. I'll start here, you begin at the other end. We'll meet in the middle." Aristotle pushed his shoulder against the door of the first warehouse. When it didn't give, he picked up a rock and smashed in the window.

Colin was already running to the far end of the row. He hoped none of the buildings were equipped with alarms, but they all looked empty, derelict. He was able to push into the first building by simply shoving in the door. Thick dust covered everything. There were no footprints in the dust, no signs of recent habitation.

He ran to the next building. This one was not so easily breached. It took him several minutes of battering the door before he gained entry. Nothing. No one had disturbed the dust in this building for a very long time either.

Where was she? He felt the first stirrings of panic. What if they were wrong? What if she wasn't here? Colin searched ever more desperately, running to the next warehouse, and the next. There was no sign of Caitlin.

One left to go. The door resisted when he shoved it.

Aristotle joined him. "Try the window."

Together they tore off the boards covering the window and climbed in.

There were footprints in the dust.

Colin didn't at first see Caitlin. When he realized she was huddled in a debris-filled corner, there he almost cried with relief. He ran to kneel beside her, gathering her limp body into his arms. "Caitlin, my darling. We're here."

She didn't respond. Her skin was a waxy color, her pulse was weak.

He looked up at Aristotle. "She's alive. But she's unconscious and there's blood on her clothing. She needs medical attention. Where are the damned police Andre promised? I have to get Caitlin to safety."

Aristotle put his hand on Colin's shoulder. "We need to go! They could return any minute."

Colin was shaking with the strain. "They've got her handcuffed to a bloody pipe."

Without a word Aristotle grabbed the pipe with both hands and pulled it out of the radiator.

Together they hurried out of the building, Colin bearing a bundle, limp and loose in his arms.

"I'll call for an ambulance." Aristotle had his phone in his hand.

Colin shook his head. "With her in this shape, the hospital's the first place they'd look for her. My aunt's a doctor and she lives about forty kilometers from here, on a farm, inland. Caitlin will be more comfortable and safer there. It's not someplace Allard and Bisset would ever think to look for her. But we need a car."

"In for a dime, in for a dollar," Aristotle said. "I'll be back with a car in five minutes."

Good to his word, he arrived back in short order with an elderly black Renault sedan. "Keep the motor running until you get to your destination. I couldn't find one with keys on this short notice."

"Aristotle, you have talents of which I was unaware." Colin eased Caitlin gently into the back seat of the car.

"An ill-spent youth. When you have her to safety, drive the car some distance away and leave it. We don't need to add car theft to our list of crimes and misdemeanors in this country."

"What about you?"

"I'm going to stay here and wait for André and the police to show up. And then I'll hitch a ride back to Paris with André. Call me and I'll fill you in and tell you where I am. Look after Caitlin."

Colin nodded. "You can be sure I will." He was several blocks away, on the outskirts of town, when he heard police sirens heading toward the warehouses.

The clock in the tower struck midnight.

Chapter Thirteen

Caitlin stirred. She was on a cloud, surrounded by clouds. All soft and comforting. She roused a little. Down, she thought. Down pillow, feather bed. Where was she? She snuggled deeper, pulling the duvet more closely around her, cozy, cocooned, and safe. If she was dreaming, she didn't want to wake up.

Nic Bisset. The name invaded her consciousness. Nic the knife. She screamed and bolted straight upright.

Instantly Colin's arms were around her. "You're safe, Caitlin. We have you. You're in a safe place." His voice broke. "I'm so sorry. I should never have let you out of my sight."

"Colin?" Tears brimmed over.

He held her tighter, fighting his own tears, as she released all her pent-up fear and terror. When she had cried herself out, Colin handed her a bunch of tissues.

She gave him a shaky "Thank you" and hiccupped.

"Water," he said. He went into the bathroom and was back a moment later with a glass in his hand. "Drink," he instructed.

Gradually her hiccups subsided. She pulled the covers out a little and looked down. She was wearing a voluminous white flannel nightgown. Whose? Pulling the neckline down, she saw a neat bandage on her right breast, where Nic had flayed a strip of skin off when Allard had Colin on the phone. She moaned as the memory of pain flashed back, making her shiver uncontrollably.

Colin held her until she stopped shaking.

"Your wounds will heal." He slid his hand down her arm. "My Aunt Adéle is a doctor. She cleaned and dressed both of them. She said they must have hurt like hell, but they won't leave much scarring."

He stood and paced. "I can't forgive myself for letting this happen. I should have been more vigilant." He stopped and shook his head. "What were you thinking, Caitlin, going out alone after all the precautions we took in the last month?"

His voice held an edge of anger Caitlin had never heard before. "You do realize you could have been killed? Your life wouldn't have been worth a sou once you were of no more use to them. Once they had the dragon."

Caitlin's eyes filled with tears again.

Colin stood and looked at her. "Stop, Caitlin. No more tears. That's enough now."

To her own surprise, the tears abruptly stopped.

"You are not to venture out alone again. Not one step outside the door. Not until Jules Allard and Nic Bisset are behind bars. Either Aristotle or I will be with you every minute of the day and night. Do you understand?" His voice held sharp command.

Meekly she nodded. No one had ever given her a direct order before. A small part of her wanted to rebel, but on the other hand—

"Good. It's settled then." Colin seemed to deflate. He sat back down on the bed as if his legs would no longer hold him. His arms came around her and he rested his head on her shoulder. She realized he was weeping silently.

She held him and caressed his hair as if he were a child. "I'm so sorry," she said. "It was a stupid, thoughtless thing to do."

"I was afraid I'd lost you," he said simply. "And I'm not sure I could have gone on living if I had."

Caitlin hid her shock at the words. She held him tight, but in her mind questions whirled. Yes, she loved him, she wanted to be with him, but she also loved her life, her work and her independence. They could not always be together. This was real life, not a fairy tale. She couldn't begin to think how there could be a "happily-ever-after" for them.

She imagined herself in living in Ireland, doing nothing but being the professor's wife. It would never work. But, oh, she did love him. She loved him more than she could ever have imagined loving anyone. And then there was his love-making. How she could live without that? But bed didn't make a life. And she loved her life as it was. Or at least as it had been before Colin Stryker strode into it.

****

Colin took a deep breath, forced himself to bring his roller-coasting emotions under control. He wanted to ask her to marry him, but he remembered Aristotle's advice. He had to wait until she was ready, until she thought it was her idea. It was hard. He wanted to grab her and take her to the church and have the priest say the words now, this minute. When he thought he'd lost her—

"Where are we?" Caitlin asked.

He tore his thoughts away from his inner vision of a world without Caitlin, and brought himself forcefully back to the present. "We're in the farm house of my aunt Adéle and my uncle Bertrand."

"Is he the one who's a chef? The one who taught you to cook?"

"One and the same. He's retired now and contents himself with cooking just for the two of them. But he's in heaven today. He's planning lunch and dinner for the four of us."

He stood. "Do you feel able to get up and dress? Come out to the kitchen and meet my aunt and uncle and have lunch? You've slept for almost twelve hours. You must be hungry. Tante Adéle has washed all your clothes and they're dry now. I'll go get them for you.

****

Caitlin leaned back against the pillows. She had no memory of those final hours in the warehouse, of her rescue, even of how she got to this sanctuary. They had drugged her again after the horrible call to Colin where Nic had flayed a piece of skin off her breast so she would scream convincingly while they had Colin on the phone. She shuddered at the memory. That Nic and Jules would have killed her once they had the dragon, she had no doubt.

Why were they doing this? Endangering all their lives for a trinket, however valuable or important a trinket it was?

But it was more than that now. It now involved the reputation of a woman whose career was cut short by its theft. It would not do to return the piece only to have it further damage Gabrielle Colbert. They had to discover who in the museum had collaborated with the thieves. And to do that they needed to continue to hide Marie Antoinette's amulet a little longer. They needed it to draw out the man behind the scenes. Who was it they suspected? Someone named Pierre Lamont? A former colleague of Gabrielle's?

Colin returned with her clothes, cutting her reverie short. "Do you need help dressing?"

"No, I can manage. I'll be out in a few minutes. I'm clean. Who bathed me?"

"Tante Adéle. I was going to, but she was adamant. I'm sure you'd feel better with a shower, but not until the dressing's ready to be changed. Until then I'm afraid it's sponge baths."

Caitlin made a face. "Okay, get out. I'll join you in a few minutes."

She had no problem finding the kitchen. She simply followed the enticing aromas.

A well-rounded woman with a pouf of white hair and a surprisingly young face came over to greet her. "I'm glad to see you up and about." She took Caitlin's two hands in her own. "I'm Colin's aunt. You may as well call me *tante;* everyone else does. Even my patients. The man stirring the sauce over there is Colin's *oncle,* Bertrand."

Bertrand, a huge man wearing a large black and white striped apron, turned toward her and smiled, saluting her with his wooden spoon. "Compliments. The lunch will be ready in moments. A *pot au feu.*"

Colin put his arm around her shoulder and squeezed her. "You're looking somewhat more yourself. May I offer you a glass of wine?" He picked up the bottle from the middle of the table.

"I think not." It was the voice of the doctor, not the aunt. "We need to make sure there are no residual effects from the drugs those two were pumping into her.

No wine for a couple of days. We'll give her some non-alcoholic cider instead."

Caitlin was relieved. She was giddy and slightly nauseated. But the heady whiff of lamb and onions and spices was making her light-headed with hunger. When was the last time she had eaten? And what had it been? She couldn't even remember.

She looked around. "Where's Aristotle?"

"Once he knew you were safe, he went back to Paris with André."

Soon they were all sitting around the table with large bowls of hearty peasant stew in front of them. She dipped into the rich brown sauce. It was wonderful. Even Colin had never made her anything as delectable.

They ate with concentration. There was little conversation beyond "pass the wine, please."

Finally, Colin pushed back his chair. "You haven't lost your touch, *oncle*. I couldn't begin to replicate your sauce."

"I should hope not. You spent your formative years buried in the past, not in the kitchen. Historian! What kind of job is that for a man, I ask you? Although I seem to recall you do pretty well in the kitchen for an amateur."

"Amateur?" Colin said. "When I apprenticed with one of the best chefs in France?"

Bertrand gave a deep rolling laugh. "I remember well when you couldn't even make a simple hollandaise sauce. But you were determined. I'll give you that. You kept at it." He turned to Caitlin. "Is he any good in the kitchen?"

"In my experience," she glanced at Colin with a smile, "only his uncle is better."

Bertrand laughed. "You have found yourself a diplomat, my boy."

Tante Adéle got up from the table and went to the huge range occupying most of one brick wall in the kitchen. Reaching into the smaller of the two ovens, she pulled out an apple tarte, its brown sugar topping bubbling. She set it on the brick counter beside the stove. "It will need to cool for a few minutes before I cut it."

She sat back down at the table. "So what is your plan? I understand everything you've told me so far, but what are you going to do about it? How are you going to resolve this? Because this young woman," she glanced at Caitlin, "is in danger as a result of your cowboy antics."

Colin frowned. "It got out of hand. It was to have been simple. We take the amulet to France, we turn it over to my curator friend, we get on the next plane back to San Francisco."

"But it didn't happen that way, did it?" Colin's aunt looked hard at him. "Things seldom work as easily as we'd like them to. So now you need a plan. What is it? I assume you have one?"

It was Caitlin who replied. "The problem, at its root, is still simple. We have to get the dragon back to where it belongs in the Louvre and find out who turned off the security system in the first place."

****

The next five days went by in a placid haze for Caitlin. As the effect of the drugs wore off, she was more like herself.

Colin had kept his distance since the first day when she had so needed his comfort. She missed his reassuring touch and his presence in her bed. Of course he would be circumspect around his aunt and uncle, but he seemed distant beyond the mere necessity for propriety. He wasn't talking to her. He wasn't including her when he spoke with Aristotle on the phone and made his plans. She didn't like being left in the dark.

She was curled up in the sunshine of a cushioned window seat looking out on the garden and the fields beyond. Sheep were grazing on a distant hillside. She had been told there was a village just five kilometers down the road, but from here, there was no other sign of human habitation. They were at the end of the world. At a blessed end of the world.

Colin came into the room. He pulled a chair up beside her.

"I love it here," Caitlin said. "I think it's the most peaceful place I've ever been."

"Good," Colin said. "Then you won't mind staying here a bit longer while I go back to Paris."

Caitlin looked at him, not comprehending.

"You're going to Paris? What about me?"

"I want you to stay here, out of the line of action. You'll be safe here. Bisset and Allard know nothing of this place."

She unfolded from her window seat. With an energy she hadn't experienced in days, she stood and put her hands on her hips. "What do you mean stay here? If you think I'm going to let you go running off to Paris to take on the bad men all by yourself, you've got another think coming! You've forgotten it's *my* dragon. And I'm going to see this thing through to the end."

Colin's mouth twitched. "I wondered what it would take to break you out of the lethargy of the last days."

Caitlin pummeled his chest with her fists. He laughed and caught them in his own and brought his mouth down to hers in a kiss claiming her as undeniably his.

"Welcome back, Caitlin. I've missed you. Of course, you'll come with me. Just as long as you promise never to venture out without one of us tagging along. We need to finish this up so you can get back to Marcus-Pfeiffer."

"Ohmygod. I haven't even thought about Marcus-Pfeiffer. It's a good thing I sent them all the pieces I had finished before we left. But I still have some of the order to complete."

"We should be able to get you home in time. As Sherlock said, 'the game is afoot.'"

****

Things moved swiftly. That afternoon they made their goodbyes to Tante Adéle and Oncle Bertrand.

"Don't forget what I said, my boy," Bertrand said. "Think about having the wedding here. Your mother can't cope with it alone. And I understand your fiancée has no family."

He turned to Caitlin, kissing her first on one cheek and then on the other. "I hope you don't mind, my dear. But a wedding is important. Family must be involved. And we're now your family."

Caitlin, flustered, found herself, for once, speechless.

They piled into the elderly Peugeot Colin's uncle had offered them for the remainder of their stay in France.

What in God's name had Colin told his aunt and uncle about their relationship? Caitlin waited until they were down the long drive and on the road. "*Wedding?*" she said, fuming, ready for a fight.

"Sorry, love. I can't imagine how they got such an idea. I'd remember if I'd asked you to marry me. And I'm quite certain I haven't."

She deflated like a balloon. No. He hadn't asked her to marry him. He'd said he loved her, but that didn't equate to a proposal of marriage. Colin was thirty-nine. He'd successfully avoided the altar for many years. And in those years there must have been other women.

She was silent on the four-hour drive to Paris.

****

Colin pulled the car into an underground garage. "We're here."

"Where is here?" Caitlin asked.

"A hotel on the outskirts of Paris. One of those chain hotels that cater to tour groups. The last place Bisset and Allard would think to look for us."

At the desk, they picked up keys for side-by-side rooms. Aristotle was already in residence.

"You get the room in the middle," Colin told her. "Between mine and Aristotle's."

He wouldn't be sleeping with her? Somehow she'd assumed once they left the home of his aunt and uncle...

They took the lift up to the fifth floor. He saw her into her room. "Do not ever open this door to anyone but Aristotle or me. Not housekeeping, not room service..." Colin took a deep breath. "Do I make myself clear?"

"Don't you dare take that tone of voice with me, Colin Stryker!"

He put a soothing hand on her shoulder. "Caitlin,

please."

She deflated. "I understand. But stop treating me as if I'm a porcelain doll. One without brains at that."

Colin sighed. "Of course. You went through hell and came back whole. You're a very strong woman, Caitlin. But I went through hell, too. And maybe, just maybe, I'm not as strong as you. And maybe I'm feeling more than a little guilt for having landed you in this precarious position."

Guilt? He thought he was somehow responsible? Her voice when she spoke was conciliatory. "I'll be careful. I'll answer the door only to you."

"Good," Colin replied. "You should be safe here. André is the only one who knows where we are. We want to keep it that way until this plays out. We can take cabs or the metro into the city center as needed. I want you to stay here tomorrow morning with Aristotle. I intend to invite Pierre Lamont to lunch. I think it's time we sized up the enemy."

Chapter Fourteen

Colin called the Louvre and asked to speak to Dr. Lamont.

A moment later, a strong male voice came on the line. "This is Pierre Lamont. How may I help you?"

"My name is Colin Stryker. I'm an historian with a particular interest in eighteenth and nineteenth century France. In my research, I've come across some interesting references to the crown jewels of the Bourbon monarchy and I'd like to discuss my findings with you. I understand you're an expert in this area?"

"I know your name, Dr. Stryker. I've read your book, *The Roots of a Republic*. It's an interesting view of the origins of the French revolution. As to the collection of crown jewels in the Louvre, yes, they are one part of my responsibility in the museum."

It struck Colin the words could have been pompous, but they weren't. They sounded like a simple statement of fact. "May I suggest we meet someplace for lunch? You'll be my guest, of course. Perhaps at *Les Deux Magots*?"

"I'd be delighted," the curator replied. "How will I know you?"

"I'm hard to miss. Red hair, red beard."

Laughter came over the line. "I shall be charmed to meet with you. Shall we say one o'clock?"

"One o'clock it is!"

Colin put his phone back in his pocket and frowned. Somehow the man had not sounded the way he expected. His response to Colin's request had held none of the arrogance Gabrielle described. Perhaps he reacted that way only toward women? Perhaps only to Gabrielle? It would be interesting to see how he'd react to Caitlin, if they ever met.

Les Deux Magots was almost full when Colin arrived. It was a popular watering hole with tourists who came to eat and drink where Gertrude Stein and Hemingway and Picasso had dined. Colin had reserved a table. He'd chosen *Les Deux Magots* assuming it would be easier to entice Lamont to a well-known and expensive restaurant. Thinking back to their brief conversation, he thought Lamont would probably have agreed to meet him anyplace. He had not needed the lure of high prices and haute cuisine.

Lamont had him off-kilter. How would he react if faced with an accusation of collusion with Bisset and Allard? With manipulating Gabrielle's enforced retirement?

"Dr. Stryker?"

Colin looked up to see a smiling face and an outstretched hand. He stood and shook the hand of the man he hoped to entrap. "Dr. Lamont."

Pierre Lamont sat in chair facing Colin. A slender figure, impeccably dressed in a dark blue suit with an understated silk tie. The picture of a career curator in a world-famous museum. He had an unlined face, open and guileless, framed by dark wavy hair.

"Shall we order first?" Colin suggested.

"By all means." Pierre Lamont studied the menu briefly. "I recommend the veal. It's done in a quite remarkable sauce here."

"Fine with me," Colin said. It seemed Lamont was no stranger to this restaurant.

Once they'd placed their order, Lamont fixed his gaze on Colin. "Now what's this all about? I'm afraid I don't buy a scholar of your stature hunting down the trivia of the jewelry of a failed monarchy."

In spite of himself Colin laughed. "Yes and no. I'm interested in the aborted robbery six years ago. And in the one who got away."

Lamont sat back in his chair. "Ah!"

"Can you tell me just what happened?"

"Please enlighten me as to why you're interested. It's an event I'd much prefer to forget." The curator gave a wintery smile.

"And yet it benefited you."

"Benefited? Oh, you mean my promotion from Associate to Curator. Yes, in a sense I suppose it did, although I had already been offered the promotion in any case. Curator in another department. And, at the time, I was considering a very good offer from the Museum of Civilization in Ottawa, as Director."

Colin raised his eyebrows. "Why did you turn down the Ottawa job? That's a very prestigious museum."

"Leave Paris for Ottawa?" He shrugged. "Need you ask? Ottawa was what you call a fallback position. When the Louvre offered me a promotion, my decision was easy. I had no desire to uproot myself, to leave Paris."

The waiter appeared with their wine and both men fell silent as Pierre Lamont went through the ritual of tasting and nodding his approval to the waiter, who then proceeded to fill both their glasses and place the bottle in a cooler beside their table.

Colin took a sip of his. "Good choice."

"It's one of my favorites."

"So you're saying that Gabrielle Colbert's departure from the Louvre had nothing to do with your promotion?"

Lamont put his glass down sharply on the table. "So that's what this is about! I take it you're a friend of Dr. Colbert's?"

"For many years. I studied under her at the Sorbonne."

"For the record, my promotion was in no way dependent on Dr. Colbert's departure. I was scheduled to take over as curator in another department within the month. When her position became empty they asked me, as a favor, to consider remaining on. It was not a promotion, merely a sideways move as curator from one department to another. I am a good scholar in my field, Dr. Stryker. Not as well-known as you perhaps, but I have a solid research and publication record. I do not need to sabotage anyone for a promotion."

Pierre Lamont's voice had not risen but had increased in intensity as he spoke. His eyes glittered with anger. He stood. "And now, if you will excuse me, I seem to have lost my appetite."

"Dr. Lamont," Colin half stood. "Please stay. I was rude, and if you wish to leave, I can't blame you. But only you can clear up a very confusing situation."

Lamont hesitated, then resumed his seat. "What is it you want to know?"

"What happened six years ago? I've read the newspaper accounts, and I've heard Dr. Colbert's version of the events of that day, but you were there also, weren't you?"

"Yes, I was."

"I believe different people often see the same event differently. I'd like to hear your perspective as to what happened. What you observed during that attempted heist."

Pierre Lamont resumed his seat just as their food arrived. "Very well. But I propose we enjoy our food first. After, I'll try to answer your questions, although I remind you, six years have passed and I may be a bit hazy on some details."

Colin, savoring the aroma of the delicate sauce on the veal dish, agreed. They made small talk during the meal. Both declined dessert.

After taking a sip of his espresso, Pierre Lamont spoke. "I suppose you know the museum was warned of the upcoming robbery attempt?"

"Yes. I understand that one of the thieves, Alain Tremont, was working with the police?"

"Just so. However, that information was known to only one person, the Director. Neither I nor Dr. Colbert was informed. It seemed a possibility one of us in the department was in league with the thieves. Someone would have to disable the alarm system. And only three people, one of whom was the Director, had that capability. That left Dr. Colbert and myself. The Director hoped to discover which of us it was."

"Only three of you? I was told a number of people had access to the security system."

"You were misinformed. Only three of us had the codes."

"But Dr. Colbert was working with the police. She

was their liaison with the museum."

"She told you that? The Director was the only liaison with the police."

Colin leaned back in shock. Gabrielle had lied to him? No, it wasn't possible. He had known her for many years. She was incapable of subterfuge. What game was Pierre Lamont playing at?

"What could Gabrielle stand to gain by consorting with thieves?" Colin shook his head. "She lived simply and within her means. She had a good salary from the museum and a comfortable inheritance from her father as well. She never wanted for anything."

"I was unaware of her financial circumstances." Lamont paused in thought. "The most common reason for crime is monetary gain, but if, as you say, she had no need for money, we are left with the second most common, *une crime passionnel*, a crime of passion."

"What are you talking about? How could a theft of jewelry from the Louvre ever be considered a crime of passion?"

"Someone disabled the alarm system. That is a fact. It is highly unlikely that person was the Director. And although I can understand your reluctance to take my word for it, I did not do so. That leaves Dr. Colbert."

"You do realize if you accuse her, and she accuses you, we are in very clouded waters."

"When you first asked me to recount the events of that day, you asked for my observations. Very well, here they are. The police were waiting and the thieves were caught in the act. One of them drew a knife and wounded a policeman. In the ensuing chaos, the third thief got away. I was watching Dr. Colbert very closely.

She knew the one who got away. I mean she knew him well. I saw the look that passed between them. I saw him blow her a kiss as he left the scene with Marie Antoinette's amulet. I'm aware my interpretation of a look passing between two people cannot be construed as evidence, but I assure you, those two knew each other, and knew each other, I suspect, intimately."

"That's ridiculous!" Colin blustered. "Alain Tremont was a young man, and Gabrielle would have been in her fifties at the time of the theft."

"She's a beautiful woman. And, I suspect, a lonely one. Surely you don't think there are never liaisons between older women and younger men?"

Colin sat back in his chair. He rubbed his forehead. Was it possible? Could Gabrielle have been involved romantically with Alain Tremont?

"I must admit your conclusions carry a certain plausibility. But there must be some other explanation. I can't imagine Gabrielle…"

"I can understand your reluctance to believe my unsubstantiated accusations. But I, too, would like this…affair…to be resolved. It hangs like a weight around my neck. It could potentially damage my career. When a crime is listed as unresolved, it affects all the innocent people who were there."

Colin studied Pierre Lamont's face. He had the look of an innocent man, but according to Caitlin, so had Alain Tremont. A man's face could conceal as easily as display.

Colin signaled the waiter for their bill. He glanced at it and proffered his credit card. The waiter raised his eyebrows at the size of the tip, and said a heartfelt "Merci, Monsieur".

The two men shook hands outside the restaurant. Colin said, "I suspect you and I may be spending some time together. Why don't we dispense with the formalities? It's Colin."

The curator smiled, extending his hand. "Pierre."

"I'll be in touch with you," Colin said.

"I look forward to hearing from you."

Colin sent a text message to Aristotle.

—*Bring Caitlin and meet me in the Luxemburg Gardens, at the pond.*—

Aristotle responded with

—*We'll be there.*—

Colin decided to walk to the gardens. That would give Aristotle and Caitlin time to make the longer journey by metro. He strolled down the Boulevard Saint Germain, deep in thought. He arrived at the gardens before Caitlin and Aristotle and chose a bench facing the large octagonal basin of water with a fountain in the center. He watched children sailing model sailboats, their mothers and nannies sitting and chatting on neighboring benches, and thought about his own life. He was nearing forty, and childless. He realized with a start he wanted children. He wanted children with Caitlin. He wanted the whole nine yards. Wife, children, a place to call home, picnics in the park, a son with whom to sail model boats. What in the name of God was happening to him?

He gazed up at the marble queens and saints on their balustrade behind the fountain and remembered their stories were seldom happy ones. He decided he much preferred the laughter of children playing. He was tired of living in the past.

"Here you are! We weren't quite sure where we

were to meet." Caitlin unabashedly hugged and kissed Colin.

He held her for a long moment. He was sure Aristotle's advice about waiting until Caitlin was ready was good advice, but his patience was wearing thin. It was hard not to give in to his urge to haul her off to the nearest church and marry her, ready or not.

Aristotle sat down on the bench beside Colin. "How did your meeting with the curator go?"

Colin took a deep breath. It was hard to say the words. Somehow saying them made the accusation more real. "He seems quite certain Gabrielle was in collusion with one of the thieves. He offered nothing that would stand up as hard evidence, but his observations about the event are compelling. Gabrielle denied his allegations when Lamont took them to the Director. What else could she do? But when the director offered her the opportunity of retiring with full benefits, she accepted without hesitation. That alone seems to point to her guilt. I don't want to believe it, but Lamont makes a very good case for her involvement. He believes Gabrielle may have known Alain Tremont. Known him well."

"What do you mean, *known him well*?" Caitlin had not taken her eyes off Colin as he spoke. "You can't believe there was anything romantic between Gabrielle and Allen?"

"We have to consider the possibility. Lamont said the look that passed between them just before Alain disappeared was"—Colin sought the right word—"intimate. And remember that when she was confronted, Gabrielle chose to retire rather than fight back. That's very unlike her."

"I don't believe it," Caitlin said. "This woman, with all her credentials and her history of service to the Louvre, was convicted with no evidence stronger than a *look* Lamont says he saw passing between her and Allen, I mean Alain? How is that possible? It's a disgrace. And if you're implying that there was something going on between them, that's ridiculous. She's far too old for him." Her voice had risen in righteous anger as she spoke.

Colin shrugged and answered mildly, "I am just recounting what Lamont told me. I am sorry if his conclusions distress you. They certainly distress me. But we must at least consider the possibility that he is correct in his assumptions, that Gabrielle was involved romantically with Alain Tremont. Whether it is true of not we have no way of knowing without confronting Gabrielle."

"But it's absurd, Colin. Allen was only thirty-four when he died. Would he have been involved romantically with a woman in her fifties?"

"You yourself commented on Gabrielle's beauty. There are numerous classic examples of relationships between older women and younger men. Cleopatra, Catherine the Great, and Elizabeth the First of England are just three of many. Besides, you're mistaken about Alain's age. The police report listed his age of death as forty-two. Not too young for Gabrielle. Although this doesn't mean I buy all that Pierre Lamont was selling."

"Forty-two?" Caitlin's looked at Colin, her eyes wide with shock. "That's not what he told me."

"That isn't the only thing he lied to you about, is it?"

Caitlin shook her head. "How could I have been so

naive?"

Aristotle, who had remained silent throughout the exchange, now put his hands on Caitlin's shoulders and spoke to her directly. "We don't expect subterfuge from those we are close to. I suspect Alain Tremont was a past master at deception. It appears his stock-in-trade was befriending women and then stealing from them."

"But he didn't steal from me."

"No." Aristotle agreed. "His friendship with you is a mystery. And another mystery is why he stole the amulet and then didn't do what any other thief would have done. He didn't break it up and sell the stones separately. He could have been living in the lap of luxury. Instead, he was living in a small apartment in Oakland and, according to the police, actually working part-time as an accountant. Was he tired of running? Did he just want a quiet, normal life? You thought he was a good man. Maybe that's what he was trying to be."

Caitlin smiled. "I'd like to believe that. It fits the Allen Thompson I knew."

Aristotle said, "I don't believe we know the truth of this yet. Try to keep an open mind. Now if you two can spare me for a few hours, I have a date and I'm going to see a bit of Paris."

Caitlin's eyebrows rose. "You have a date? With a girl?"

"Of course with a girl." Aristotle gave them a look that said *no more questions*. With a wave, he turned and strode toward the park entrance and the metro station.

"Well!" Caitlin let out her breath. "That's the first time I've ever known Aristotle to have a date in the five years I've known him."

"About time, I'd say," Colin replied. "Now can you think of any way we could while away the time until he returns?"

Caitlin looked up at Colin and smiled. "I think we can amuse ourselves in his absence."

Chapter Fifteen

Stretching her arms above her head, Caitlin turned to a drowsy Colin and said, "We've been in France for ten days and I've seen nothing of Paris."

He propped up on one elbow. "What would you like to see?"

"Everything! The Eiffel Tower and the Arc de Triomphe, and the Tuileries gardens and Monet's water lilies and Rodin's *the Kiss* and the Musee d'Orsay and…"

Colin interrupted. "I don't believe we can do that all in one afternoon. But we can make a good beginning." He gave her a smack on the behind. "Go get dressed. Ten minutes?"

She in turn, gave him a long, lingering kiss.

"Get out of bed now, Caitlin, or I won't be responsible for what happens next. I can assure you we won't be seeing anything of Paris."

She rolled over and off the bed. "Ten minutes to shower and dress."

****

They took the metro to the Champ de Mars stop. As Caitlin emerged from the underground into the sunlight of a warm May day, she gazed, entranced, at the gigantic steel lattice-like structure that was the Eiffel Tower.

"It's so big," she said. "Somehow I never realized

just how tall it was."

"More than a thousand feet. It was the tallest building in the world when it was built for the 1889 World's Fair. Parisians at that time hated it. They were appeased only by assurances that it would be dismantled immediately after the fair."

"Dismantled? You mean torn down? Destroyed? It's the symbol everyone associates with Paris. How could they ever have considered tearing it down?"

"Parisians hated it looming over their beautiful eighteenth century houses, their marble monuments and their ancient churches. They hated the way it dominated the skyline."

"Then how come it's still standing?"

"Gustave Eiffel was a very clever man. He found practical uses for it. Reasons for stretching out its life; there's a radio antenna on the top, for instance. Very useful during two world wars. Eventually Parisians came to accept it and then to take ownership of it as a unique symbol of their city."

"I want to climb the stairs," Caitlin said. "I don't want to wait in line for the elevator."

"Cait, are you out of your mind! There are 1710 steps, 360 just to the first floor, and 1060 more to the second!

"I don't care."

Colin sighed. "I guess that's what I get for falling in love with a younger woman. Okay, off we go."

At about halfway up to the first level, as they paused to get their breath, Colin said, "You were right. This way we have interesting views over the city, and a much greater sense of the genius of the construction."

At the first level Colin asked, "Would you like to

eat in the restaurant here? It's a very good one."

Caitlin hesitated for only a moment. "No. I'd rather spend our time seeing things. But we don't need to climb any higher. What's next?"

"Well, we're not far from Musee d'Orsay. Are you up for a large dose of the Impressionists?"

"My favorites. Monet, Van Gogh, Degas."

As they strolled hand in hand along the riverside, Colin had the uneasy feeling someone was following them. He stopped, looking around as if to enjoy the view of the river. About a block away—was or was not the man, the one with his back to them studying posters on a kiosk, Jules Allard? How could he have found them so easily in this big city? Colin looked the other way and saw a Metro sign. A good place to get rid of his follower, if indeed they were being followed.

He said nothing to Caitlin of his suspicions. They continued to stroll along the sidewalk above the Seine. At the entrance to the Metro he put his arm around her shoulder and hurried her down the steps. "Jump!" he ordered as they approached the turnstile. A confused Caitlin did as instructed, Colin right behind her. He pushed her along the platform, running, staying close behind her, his body a shield to anyone following them. A train was just pulling in. He guided Caitlin hurriedly through the disembarking crowd, onto the train, and took a window seat, where he scanned the crowd moving to get on.

There he was, the bastard. Jules Allard was pushing his way into their car. How the hell had he located them? He wished Caitlin weren't with him. He'd like to get his hands on Jules, but he couldn't put Caitlin at risk again. There was no time to lose. He took

Caitlin firmly by the arm and threaded their way through the crowded car to the other end. Just as the doors were closing he pushed her through them, following her onto the platform. Jules' angry face peered at them through a window as the train pulled out.

Colin pulled Caitlin up the steps, back into the bright sunlight.

"What was all that about?" Caitlin asked.

"We were being followed. I've shaken him for the moment, but I'm afraid our day of sight-seeing is over."

Caitlin shivered involuntarily.

Colin's arms came tight around her. "It's okay. We lost him." He hailed a taxi and gave the address of their hotel.

Settling back into the seat Caitlin asked, "How did they find us?"

"I can't imagine. I guess they've somehow traced us to our hotel and they've been watching us come and go. We're going to have to change hotels again immediately."

Back in their rooms, they threw their belongings into their backpacks and did the same with Aristotle's. Colin sent a text message to Aristotle, telling him they were moving.

Aristotle's immediate response was

—*Meet us at Celine's flat. It's in the Troisieme Arrondisment, the Marais, 13 rue Francois Miron. She's on the fifth floor. Make sure you're not followed, and tell no one. No one.*—

—*See you there in an hour*—Colin texted back.

With their bags slung over their shoulders, they settled their hotel bill and walked out of the hotel.

Ignoring the taxis parked in front, Colin led Caitlin down the street and around the block to a taxi stand.

"Gare du Nord," he instructed the driver.

"Are we leaving Paris?" Caitlin asked. Where are we going?"

Colin held up his hand, a signal not to talk in front of the taxi driver.

Caitlin settled back in her corner of the taxi.

At the train station, Colin handed the taxi driver fifteen euros and guided Caitlin through the doors into the crowded terminal. He headed across to the Metro entrance and pulled her along, down the steps through the turnstile, this time prepared with tickets. They boarded a train headed for the Marais district.

Fifteen minutes later, they emerged at the *Rue de Rivoli.*

"It's just a block or so from here. You okay?" Colin had his hand under Caitlin's arm, hurrying her along.

"I'm so tired of this, Colin. I just want it over."

"We're going make that happen, Cait. I agree, every moment we continue to hold this accursed amulet is a danger to you. I'm not willing to put you at risk for a trinket, however valuable. But there is only one public entrance to the Louvre. And if Jules followed us to the Eiffel Tower, you can bet Nic was waiting and watching the entrance to the Louvre, knife in hand. We have a plan. It will just take a couple more days to get fully organized."

He stopped in front of a building housing a bakery on the ground floor and knocked on a sturdy wooden door to one side of the bakery entrance. When no one answered, he pushed it open.

An elderly woman sat knitting on a chair just inside the door. She looked askance at him.

Colin addressed her. "Bonjour, Madam. We're here to see Celine Colbert. She's on the fifth floor?"

The woman nodded disinterestedly, muttered, "Lift isn't working today," and returned to her knitting. Caitlin and Colin climbed the steps that surrounded an old, and at this moment, dysfunctional, lift.

The door flew open before they could knock.

Celine greeted them with a wide smile. "I'm so glad Aristotle thought of having you stay with us. I've barely seen anything of you, Colin!" She turned and included Caitlin in her smile. "And I'm looking forward to getting to know you better, Caitlin. Aristotle has told me so much about you and about your wonderful designs. Come in, come in."

Caitlin was trying to absorb the "us" in Celine's greeting. How could things have progressed so far between Aristotle and Celine without her even noticing? They were now an "us"? A twinge of something she refused to acknowledge as jealousy clawed at her. Her Aristotle, her brother, her friend and companion for the last five years, was involved with this strange young Frenchwoman with the purple hair? With someone he'd known for less than ten days? How could that be?

Celine stepped back so they could enter the loft.

It was an attic room, one large open space. A tiny kitchen graced one corner, with a table dressed, Provençal style, in blue and white with a pattern of sunflowers splashed across it. A bowl of haphazardly arranged daffodils sat in the center. A comfortable-looking sofa was nearby. Tucked under the eaves on the other side of the room, a double bed was piled high with pillows. It was a thoroughly inviting looking space, homey and attractive. It somehow suited Celine.

"I apologize for the flea market furniture. It's all I can afford right now. My mother offered to furnish it for me, but I wanted to do it myself."

"It's charming," Caitlin replied.

"You and Colin can have the bed. Aristotle and I will make do with the sofa. It's not too bad. Sorry for the lack of privacy. But I think we can be pretty sure they won't trace you here."

A few minutes later, the four of them were sitting around the table with tiny cups of espresso in front of them.

Caitlin only half heard the conversation. Her mind was still chewing on the idea of Aristotle and Celine.

Aristotle looked at her with a grin and answered her unasked questions. "Yes, I've been seeing quite a bit of Celine on those long afternoons when you and Colin were otherwise occupied. And yes, it's serious. She's quite a girl. Did you know it's her ambition to be a jewelry designer, like you?"

"Is that so?" She turned to Celine. "I thought you were in sales." Caitlin kept her voice neutral. She had thought of Aristotle as hers for years. Her friend, her only family. And now there was someone else in his life. She was finding it a little difficult to accept.

"I do what I must to make a living," the younger woman answered with a shrug.

Aristotle continued. "She's the Paris sales rep for a jewelry company in Nice. Their pieces are very different from yours. She showed me some. They're hard to describe. Very modern. Think Picasso's cubist period. Celine isn't all that crazy about them." He reached across the table and took Celine's small hand in his two large ones. "She just needs a chance to work with the right teacher." He looked pointedly at Caitlin.

Caitlin absorbed the suggestion but wasn't quite ready to answer it. "So what do we do now?" she asked. "We can't spend the rest of our lives hiding out here."

"Were you able to complete the arrangements we discussed?" Colin asked Celine.

"No problem. I still have quite a number of friends at the Sorbonne. The date is set, the banners are ready and everyone is looking forward to it. It should be fun."

Colin sighed. "I hope it doesn't prove dangerous. I don't want anyone hurt over this. I intend to work closely on it with my friend in the Paris police on it."

"Your undercover cop friend, André?" Aristotle asked.

"Right. Couldn't do it without him. But before I let him know what we're planning, I need to speak with Gabrielle again. I can't just ignore Pierre Lamont's conclusions."

"Of course you can't," Celine replied. "But my mother gained nothing by that theft five years ago."

"I know, Celine." Colin shook his head. "She lost her career over it. Have you spoken to her recently?"

"A couple of days ago. There's something wrong with her, Colin. There's been something wrong for a long time. She won't talk to me about it, but something is eating at her. And I don't think it's just the loss of her career. She has lost weight. She no longer takes pride in her appearance."

"She looked fine the day we saw her," Caitlin interjected.

"She made a special effort the day you came over, but there are days when she doesn't even get out of bed. She's been increasingly depressed. She won't talk to me about it, and she ignores my suggestions when I ask her to see a doctor. It's getting worse. I hope you can get to the bottom of it, Colin. I'm worried sick about her."

Colin reached across the table and patted her hand. "I'll do what I can."

Celine took a shuddering breath. "Do you think my mother could have known something about that theft at the Louvre six years ago, Colin? It all began about then."

Caitlin interrupted. "Nonsense! Colin is trying to clear your mother's name. The most likely collaborator is Pierre Lamont."

"It doesn't seem possible your mother could have been involved with the likes of Allard and Bisset," Colin added. "Why would she lie to us now about what happened six years ago? She has nothing left to lose."

Aristotle added, "Your mother comes under suspicion only because of what Pierre Lamont said. But is he telling us the truth? Is he as straightforward as Colin thinks he is?"

Colin pushed his cup of now-cold coffee away. "I no longer know what or who to believe. Was Pierre Lamont involved in the theft? He makes a very plausible case that he was not. If we are to believe him, we are left with your mother, Celine." He hesitated. "What do you remember about her private life at that time? Who was she seeing? Could she have been involved with Alain Tremont?"

"There was a man. But his name wasn't Tremont. I

only met him a few times. He seemed quite charming. Alexandre somebody or other, I forget his last name."

"I'll be seeing your mother tomorrow morning. We need to know the facts. Whatever she may have done in the past, she is still my friend. I want to help her."

"And she is my mother, no matter what she's done. We need the truth between us so she can heal."

Caitlin shook her head. "I thought you were going to clear her name, Colin. You said the most likely inside man was Pierre Lamont."

Colin sighed. "I admit to being confused. Was Pierre Lamont involved in the theft? He makes a very plausible case that he was not the inside man. If we are to believe him, that leaves only Gabrielle. I've put off talking to her for too long. Was she involved with Alain Tremont? Did she give him the information they needed to set up that robbery? Was she acting as liaison with the police, as she told us? Lamont says not. These are questions only Gabrielle can answer."

Caitlin banged her hand down on the table and burst into tears. "I don't care. I just want to get the dragon back to where it belongs. I've been drugged, kidnapped, assaulted, and put in danger for my life. I'm sick of all this. Tomorrow I'm going to march into the front door of the Louvre and into the head honcho's office and hand the dragon over to him. After that, it's over to someone else to sort out. I'm going home."

"Patience, Caitlin. We do have a plan." Colin rested his calming hands on her shoulders.

Aristotle offered her his red handkerchief. "But I think the less you know in advance, the better. Our plan skirts the law rather closely."

She wiped her eyes. "Why am I not surprised?"

Chapter Sixteen

The next morning, armed with croissant and beignet, Colin knocked at Gabrielle's door.

She answered, dressed in cream linen pants and a loose blue silk shirt. After the usual kisses on each cheek, she took the package of pastries from Colin and indicated they should sit at the miniscule table where she customarily took her meals, meals she had shared many times in the past with Colin.

"I'll get us a coffee," she said, moving into her kitchen. Looking at her critically, Colin could see how loose her clothes hung on her frame. She was thin to the point of being frail. How could he not have seen that before?

She poured them each a small cup of the dark brew and sat down facing him.

Colin studied his friend's face. She looked haggard, as if she had not slept well in a very long time. She had aged overnight. Lines of worry traced her brow.

Gabrielle took a sip of coffee and set the cup carefully back in its saucer. "You know, don't you? I was afraid once you investigated my secret would be out."

"Why did you do it?" His voice was mild. "What were you thinking, Gabrielle?"

"I've been such a fool. Please, Colin, Celine

mustn't know. She's all I have left in the world. I couldn't bear to lose her."

"Celine understands more than you give her credit for. She's a warm and intelligent young woman, and she loves you deeply. She'd never turn her back on you." Colin sighed. "Start from the beginning. It was Alain Tremont, wasn't it? You were lovers."

"I never knew him as Alain Tremont. To me he was Alexandre Trouville. He brought love into my life at an age when I was afraid I might never find it again. I was desperately lonely. Can you understand? At fifty-five I fell passionately in love. Oh, I'd had affairs, as you were aware, but they never touched me deeply. Until Alexandre. It was like a sickness. I simply lost all control. I was incapable of rational thought."

"Love can do that to you. What did Celine think of him?"

"Celine was happy for me, and I think she liked Alexandre. But she was working on her master's at the College of Art, and was seldom home. She never knew the truth about him. I'd like to keep it that way if I can. She assumed the affair had run its course when he disappeared from our lives."

"I'll keep your secrets if I can, Gabrielle, but at present they're endangering Caitlin's life. That's not acceptable. I'll do whatever I have to, to remove that danger. Tell me the rest of it. What happened to make you willing to risk everything you'd worked for in your professional life?"

"When we met he told me he was in the jewelry business." She gave a bitter laugh. "We'd been living together for eight months before he told me just *how* he was in the jewelry business. Eight months during which

I had become emotionally dependent on him. By then if he had told me he was the devil incarnate I wouldn't have cared. I loved him, whoever he was, whatever he'd done."

"And then?" Colin took a sip of his now-cold coffee and pushed it away.

"One day he told me he was working with two other men on a job that would set him up for life, if I'd just cooperate. All I had to do was disable the security system, a matter of two minutes. I was appalled when he first suggested it, but he could be very persuasive." Gabrielle looked down at her hands, clenched tightly in her lap. "He told me if I did this, he'd retire and we could be together for the rest of our lives. That we could live comfortably in Brazil, or the Far East. Someplace where there were no extradition laws."

Colin pushed his chair back, incredulous. "And you were willing to do this? You believed him?"

"Ridiculous, isn't it?"

"The man was a user. He may well have had this job in the back of his mind when he first approached you."

Gabrielle's voice was barely a whisper. "I know. I know that now. It's a bitter pill to swallow."

"The two men he was working with, Nic Bisset and Jules Allard, did you ever meet them?"

"No, I never met them or even knew their names, until I read them in the newspapers after the theft. Alexandre"—Gabrielle shook her head—"I just can't think of him as Alain even now, asked me to disable the alarms. And, eventually, he wore me down. I agreed to do it."

"And then?"

"The police were there waiting. I wasn't expecting that, although from subsequent events, I gather Alexandre was. One of the other thieves pulled a knife on an officer and managed to wound him. In the ensuing chaos, Alexandre simply walked away. He turned to me and blew me a kiss as he left. He must have had the Marie Antoinette amulet on him, but I didn't know that at the time. That was the last I ever saw of him."

Tears trickled down her cheeks. "For weeks, months, I kept waiting. I was so sure he'd let me know where he was, that he would call me to join him. Hope dies hard."

****

Back at Celine's flat, Colin took Caitlin in his arms and held her, cradling her head against his shoulder. "Where are Aristotle and Celine?"

"Out, marketing for tonight's dinner."

He gave a shuddering sigh, then released her and walked across to the stare out the window at the street below. With his back to her he said, "Love can be hell."

"What happened?"

"She admitted being the inside contact for the thieves. Gabrielle disabled the alarm."

"But why? I just don't understand." Caitlin walked over to him and put her hand on his back, willing him to turn to her, to explain.

He turned, encircled her with his arms, and rested his cheek on her hair, inhaling its clean fresh smell. It always smelled faintly of vanilla. He loved the scent of her hair. "Love can be a bitch. It nearly wrecked me twenty years ago, and now it's destroying a woman I revere and respect. A woman who's been one of my closest friends for many years."

"Gabrielle?"

"When I wanted nothing except darkness and the cessation of pain, she wouldn't let me stop living. Gabrielle brought me back from hell. She forced me to go on living, she pushed me into the life of an academic, where I could bury myself in work and forget everything else. In many ways, I owe to her what and who I am today. In a sense, she freed me so I could find life again, find you, love you."

Caitlin was silent for a moment. "Allen. She did it for Allen?"

He gave a bitter laugh. "To you he was Allen Thompson, to the police he's Alain Tremont and to Gabrielle he was Alexandre Trouville. She was desperately in love with him, and he literally blew her off with a kiss as he walked out of that museum with several million dollars' worth of jewels in his pocket. She kept expecting to hear from him, waiting for him to call or write asking her to join him where ever he was."

"How sad for her. And all the while he was in California, trying to talk me into letting him move in with me, the bastard. I'm so sorry for her. How she must have suffered all these long years, waiting for a message that never came. A message he never had any intention of sending. He was a user."

A new thought occurred. "I wonder how many women he used in California before me." She frowned, "And what was he using me for?"

"A safe house, a bolt hole, I suspect. Suburban Berkeley would have been an unlikely place for his former colleagues to find him."

"But they did find him."

"Yes."

"So what are you going to do about Gabrielle? Not go to the police, I hope."

"Police? No. Of course not." Colin said. "What would be gained by that? She's already lost her position. She's lost her place in the museum world. What could be worse punishment than that?"

"Losing the man you love. Discovering you have been used. Being discarded when you're no longer useful. Those are all worse than losing a job, no matter how prestigious."

"Of course you're right." He sighed and sat down on the bed, pulling Caitlin down with him.

"We'll have to tell Aristotle and Celine, but it shouldn't go any further," she said as he gently pushed her back onto the pillows.

"Right." He nibbled her earlobe as his hands wandered down her body, tingling and arousing wherever they touched. "I love the way you smell. Don't ever change whatever it is."

"It's just soap, silly."

He unzipped her jeans and pushed his hand inside, cupping her, pressing down.

"Ahhh." She writhed. "Stop, Colin! Aristotle and Celine could be back any minute!"

"Then I'll just have to be quick, won't I?" He pushed her jeans and panties farther down so that they trapped her legs. It no longer mattered they might well have an audience before they finished.

****

At dinner that night, they waited until they had eaten the last scrumptious bite of their chicken prepared Provençal style, with tomatoes and black olives, before pushing their chairs back to discuss the situation over their espressos.

His voice flat and emotionless, Colin brought Aristotle and Celine up to date. "Your mother's greatest fear has been that you might find out," he said to Celine.

"I knew something was terribly wrong." Celine's eyes glistened with unshed tears. "I'll go to her tomorrow morning. How could she think I wouldn't understand?"

Aristotle took Celine's hand. "Perhaps now the healing can begin."

"I hope so," Celine said. "If the accomplice behind the scenes was my mother, is there any reason you can't just go to the Louvre now and hand the dragon over to the Director?"

"My point exactly." Caitlin smiled at Celine; help from an unlikely quarter. "Why couldn't we just walk into the museum like any tourist and give the amulet back now?"

"Only the fact that one or more of us could be stabbed or otherwise disabled in the process." Colin's voice was brittle. "Have you forgotten that Jules and Nic are still at large? Do you think, for one instant, they haven't got the entrance to the Louvre under surveillance? They won't hesitate to kill any or all of us if we attempt to enter the museum. And we'd have to navigate long lines at the entrance. Even with prepaid tickets we'd be stuck in a line, sitting ducks for those two."

"There is another entrance." Caitlin screwed up her face trying to remember what she had observed on that long ago first morning in Paris, before her abduction.

"A door along the side of the building facing the Seine. It's not a public entrance, but if we let Pierre Lamont know in advance, maybe he could be at that door to let us in."

"You cannot be involved in this, Caitlin." Colin's voice was definitive.

Caitlin's chin rose. "I am involved. And I will be there. And I will hand over that dragon."

"Come on, Colin," Aristotle said. "Using the side door, Caitlin should be safe if the diversion we're planning at the main entrance works."

Colin sighed. "I suppose you're right. It's just that I live in perpetual terror of losing Caitlin. If I could, I'd hide her away in a convent until this was all over."

Caitlin burst out laughing. "Colin, really! A convent?"

"It's what would have been done in the sixteenth century to protect an endangered maiden."

"An endangered maiden?" Caitlin was off in a paroxysm of laughter.

Aristotle and Celine guffawed, leaning on each other for support.

Even Colin joined in the hilarity. Wiping tears of laughter away, he said, "Sorry. It's what comes of living in the past."

Aristotle brought them all back to the seriousness of their situation. "There's one flaw in our plan."

"Only one?" Caitlin was off again, giggling. "That will be an improvement!"

Aristotle continued, ignoring Caitlin. "Sorry, Colin, but I don't trust your friend André. Every time we've needed police help, he's let us down."

"What?"

Aristotle shrugged. "Think about it, Colin. Only five people knew our whereabouts. You, me, Celine, Caitlin, and André. Somehow, Allard and Bisset knew where we were at all times. I'm pretty sure none of us told them. That leaves your friend André."

"It couldn't have been André. I've known him for years."

"Consider the chain of recent events," Aristotle said. "There were never any police about when we needed them. Did you ever *hear* André asking for police assistance?"

Colin thought back to the various times André had said he was calling for police help. "In Paris, he left his office and then came back saying the police had been put on the look-out for the car carrying Caitlin."

"And no help arrived." Aristotle continued. "It's hard to believe the Paris police are so incompetent they can't find a specific car on a specific route at a specific time. And then in Concarneau and Pont Aven, the police impeded rather than assisting us. We got arrested. Where was André then? It was hours before we got out of that shambles."

"He did rescue us, eventually."

"True. But not until Allard and Bisset had plenty of time to get away with Caitlin again. He let us stew for three hours before coming to our aid. Then he suggested we should return to Paris, and 'leave it to the police.'"

"He did, didn't he?" Colin mused. "And when he went off for police help in Concarneau, they didn't arrive until after midnight. Caitlin might have been dead by then if we hadn't rescued her on our own." Colin's voice had slowed as he spoke.

"Then there was the afternoon you were followed from the hotel to the Eiffel Tower. No one knew where we were staying except André."

Colin shook his head. "What possible reason could André have for betraying us?"

"You said he was the officer in charge at the time of the original theft?"

"Yes, he was," Colin said, "but you can't seriously believe he was involved in it!"

"I don't know," Aristotle replied. "There were entirely too many coincidences in this whole sequence of events for me. Did you give André this address?"

"No. You specifically said 'tell no one.' And I did take precautions coming here. I don't think we were followed." Colin sighed. "It's a twisted mess. Who's telling the truth? I've known André for years. What would he have to gain by double-crossing us?"

"We'll know soon enough if he's bent." Aristotle said. "I think I know a way we can entrap him. Here's what we'll do…"

****

Nic was at the entrance to the Louvre, as he had been at opening hour every day for the past week, when a young boy approached him. "You Nic Bisset?"

Nic looked at him suspiciously. "What's it to you?"

"A man paid me five euros to give this note to Nic Bisset. You Nic Bisset?"

Nic grabbed the boy by his collar. "What man?"

The boy looked over his shoulder. "I dunno. A man over there. Gone now."

Nic took the proffered note and pushed the boy away. He opened the folded note, neatly typed, "New information. We must meet. *Bistro Europa*, 8 pm. A."

Jules arrived with two steaming cups of coffee to find Nic holding the note, looking puzzled. "What do you make of this?" he said, handing the scribbled note to Jules.

"Something must have come up. He never contacts us unless it's important."

"Yes. But then he usually just calls us."

"Maybe his phone has been compromised. Maybe he's worried about security. We won't know until we see him."

****

André came strolling into police headquarters. The man at the front desk said, "Some dirty little kid came in a few minutes ago and left a note for you. I asked him who it was from, but he scampered away before I could get him."

"No problem, Honoré. You know I have a more than a few unsavory contacts. They're inclined to distrust uniforms. I'll deal with it."

He went into his office and opened the folded scrap of dirty paper. He read the message hastily scrawled in pencil, "Something's come up. Must meet. *Bistro Europa*, 8 pm. J & N."

****

At the apartment Colin paced, waiting for Celine to return.

Before she could even take off her hat and coat he asked, "Has the boy delivered the notes as planned?"

"Of course. No problem. But I still don't see how having them meet is going to tell us anything."

"It won't. As an undercover cop, André would get such messages from time to time. He'll follow it up even if he has no idea what it's about or who sent it."

204

"Why do it then?" Caitlin asked. "What do we gain by having them meet?"

"If he's not involved with them, he should arrest them on the spot. He's a police officer and they're wanted for murder and arson, not to mention abduction. His reaction when they meet will tell us a lot."

"And I chose this meeting place, this bistro for a reason," Celine said. "I know the owner, Jean-Luc. I'm going to sit at a nearby table behind a potted palm and listen to every word they say."

Aristotle continued, "We're hoping we'll be able tell from what they say whether André was involved in the original theft, whether we can trust him."

"We'll just have to wait and see how it plays out," Caitlin said. "But I don't like leaving Celine exposed."

"Help won't be far away. Jean-Luc has agreed to let Aristotle be stationed behind the kitchen door."

"And us?" Colin asked.

"Sorry, Colin. With your size and your red hair and beard? You're not easy to hide. And we don't want Caitlin anywhere near that pair. I'm afraid you two will just have to wait it out here. We'll call you the minute it's over."

****

Celine and Aristotle came down the alley and in through the kitchen door of the *Bistro Europa* at 7:30.

"Aristotle, this is my good friend Jean-Luc," Celine introduced the chef. "He knows what we're about and has agreed to help us."

The two men shook hands.

"I've put a reserved sign on their table," Jean Luc explained to Aristotle. "And Celine's table is close by, but there's a large potted palm between them.

Hopefully, they won't notice her."

Aristotle pushed open the swinging door to the dining room and studied the arrangement. "That should work," he said. "But just in case there's any problem, I'd like to sit here near the door, where I can hear what's going on. I want to be able to reach Celine in a hurry if anything goes south."

"Of course," said the chef. "As long as you're out of the way of the waiters coming and going. While you're sitting there, you must try some of my bouillabaisse."

"I hope you're going to put some of that on my table," Celine quipped, sniffing the aromatic seafood concoction.

"Of course, *ma petite.*" The chef laughed. "But now I think you must take your places before the drama begins."

Celine was at her table watching warily when, at eight o'clock on the dot, Jules and Nic arrived, and were shown to the reserved table. She could see them through the potted palm as they fidgeted with the menu the waiter thrust into their hands.

When the waiter hovered, Jules said, "We're not ready to order. We're waiting for someone."

It was eight-thirty before Andre joined them.

Celine leaned closer so as not to miss a single word.

"Where the hell were you?" Nic hissed, his impatience showing in every syllable. "I thought you said eight o'clock!"

"I was across the street making sure we didn't have any unwelcome visitors." André pulled out a chair and sat down. "You know I don't like meeting this way. So

I'm here now. What's so urgent? You know something I should know? The whereabouts of the dragon?"

"What do you mean, what do we know? You're the one who called this meeting!"

"I called...? *Merde*! I'm out of here." André knocked over his chair in his hurry to get away.

Celine got up quietly and went into the kitchen. "We've got him! Let's get back to the flat. I can't wait to see Colin's face!"

Chapter Seventeen

In Celine's flat, Caitlin paced, her nerves stretched taut with fear. Celine had no idea how dangerous Bisset and Allard were. She would be in peril every moment she was near them. Aristotle, in the restaurant kitchen, might not get to her in time to help if Nic should see her listening to them. And while Caitlin had somewhat distrusted Celine at first—that wasn't the truth. She hadn't distrusted Celine, she'd been jealous of her. Jealous because Aristotle was interested in someone else. When she should have been glad for him, instead she'd been almost rude to Celine. That would not happen again. If they all got out of this alive, she'd be kinder. She'd try to be a better person.

She stopped behind Colin's chair. He was immersed in a thick tome on the Middle Ages in France. She put her head down on his and brought her arms around him.

He reached around and pulled her down into his lap. "Nervous, love?"

"I'm worried about Celine. I've seen what those two can do."

"She has lots of protection. It's not just Aristotle. Every waiter in the restaurant has been put into the picture. She'll be safe."

"I hope so. I'm so tired of this, Colin. When will it all be over?"

"In two days, if everything goes as planned."

The door burst open and Celine and Aristotle came in, bringing the chill night air with them. Celine was laughing. "That was quite an adventure," she said, tossing her knit cap on the coat rack in the corner. "They never even noticed me."

"That's a good thing." Caitlin rushed over to Celine and hugged her. "I'm glad you're back safely. We were worried. So what happened?"

"The two were there exactly on time. They were very nervous, looking all around. I don't think they noticed me. I had my head down over my bowl of bouillabaisse. It was delicious, by the way. We should go back there when this is all over."

"Celine!" Caitlin was almost shouting. "What happened?"

"Well," Celine said, "they came in and sat down and told the waiter they'd order later. And then nothing happened for a half hour. I figured maybe André wasn't coming. That would have told us that perhaps our suspicions were unjust. But then at 8:30 on the dot he came in."

"Could you hear what they were saying?"

"There was some mix-up about who asked who to meet. I heard the words 'the dragon.' And then Andre got up and left in a hurry."

"I don't see how this puts us any farther ahead," Caitlin said.

"It does," Colin assured her. "André responded to their summons. He recognized those two criminals who are on wanted lists in two countries, and instead of arresting them on the spot, he got out of there post haste. He saw the trap and didn't want to get caught in it. We now know what we need to know. André is not to be trusted."

Aristotle went to the stove and put water and coffee in the espresso machine. "That means we can now proceed with the rest of our plan. But there won't be any police protection. We can't go to the police with this and hope word of it won't somehow filter down to André."

Caitlin thought for a moment. "If we don't tell André something about our plans for returning the amulet, he may get suspicious."

The others were silent for a moment. Celine took down four espresso cups and put them on the table. "I think André may have more to worry about than when we're returning the amulet."

The other three swiveled to stare at Celine.

"What have you done?" Aristotle asked.

Celine held up her cell phone for them to see. They saw Jules and Nic seated at the restaurant table. André came in. They could hear the short conversation clearly. Except for a brief mention of the dragon, nothing the three said was incriminating, but André's mere presence there with two wanted criminals and his hasty departure were.

"I posted this on Facebook," Celine said, "with a message identifying André Bergère as a policeman and the two men he was meeting with as Nic Bisset and Jules Allard, wanted on charges of abduction, arson, and murder."

"You didn't!" Aristotle was appalled at the risk she'd taken. "What if you'd been seen?"

"I wasn't. And then I called the office of the Commissaire of Police to be sure they saw it."

The table exploded in laughter.

Colin wiped his eyes. "I suspect we won't have to worry very much about André in the future. Talk about poetic justice!"

"So when does it happen?" Caitlin asked.

"It's set for tomorrow morning." Colin opened a package of sweet biscuits and put them on a plate in the middle of the table. "It just all came together yesterday, and until we knew whether we could trust André, we couldn't give the go-ahead to everybody involved."

"That's Tuesday," Aristotle said to Colin. "Just to be on the safe side, you should call André and tell him Caitlin will be returning the dragon on Wednesday. That way, if he hasn't been put out of commission yet, he'll be planning for the wrong day."

"Good idea." Colin took out his phone and dialed André's number. "No answer. I'll try later."

Celine added, "I suspect the police will arrive once we get there, whether we want them or not. We don't need André for that. And it won't be undercover cops, it will be the riot squad. They're the uniformed branch who usually deal with demonstrations."

"Demonstrations?" Caitlin queried.

After they described their plan to Caitlin, she laughed aloud. "Whose idea was this?"

"The original plan was mine," Colin replied, "but I couldn't have managed it without Celine and her mother. Celine persuaded some friends at the Sorbonne to help us create a fake demonstration, and Gabrielle agreed to inform her friends among newspaper and television reporters, so they'll be there early tomorrow morning. It should be fun."

"And what will I be doing?" Caitlin asked.

"What you've been wanting to do all along. You'll be returning the dragon to the Director of the Louvre."

****

Back in his office, André replayed the scene in his mind. Had he said anything incriminating? No, he didn't think so. What had they talked about? *He'd asked about the dragon. Merde!*

Who could have planned this entrapment? Not the law. Not a meeting with two wanted criminals. He'd better try to do some damage control. But how?

His phone rang.

It was Colin. "I thought you'd want to know it's all set for us to return the dragon on Wednesday morning at eight o'clock, before the museum opens. The director will meet us at the front entrance. Can you help us with some police back-up?"

"Of course. Glad to help. I'll see you there." André closed his phone and swore under his breath. Bloody hell, what should he do now? Bisset and Allard wouldn't be at the Louvre until opening time, at nine. He'd have to let them know what was coming down and when.

Or did he?

Maybe this was his opportunity to get out from under this whole mess. It had been a fiasco from the very start. Alain Tremont was supposed to have taken the Regent Diamond. Even if one discounted its historic value, once having adorned Marie Antoinette's hat and later having been set in Napoleon's sword, at 141 carats, the Regent's value was enormous. And they'd had a private buyer for it lined up, waiting in the wings. Instead, Alain had grabbed a trinket worth far less. Even if the little dragon had been broken up and its stones sold separately, they'd have realized only a pittance compared to what they'd have gotten from the sale of the Regent. But they didn't get even that pittance. Alain had fled with the dragon, and effectively disappeared.

He'd known it was a mistake when Alain suggested they use Allard and Bisset. Complete clowns. He couldn't understand, even now, why Alain had thought they needed them. He'd said they would "provide a diversion" while he got away. That "diversion" had involved wounding a fellow officer, a friend of André's. He was lucky Allard and Bisset hadn't turned evidence on him when they were convicted. Of course, that was only because they'd counted on their silence getting them their cut when they got out of jail. But there was no "cut" to get. Alain had disappeared and that was the last of it.

Until they tracked him down in California. Poor devil. He wouldn't wish a death like that on his worst enemy.

Was he willing to blow his career over that bauble? No, he was not. What should he do? Still mulling the problem over, he walked up the steps to the Commissaire's office.

"He in?" André asked the officer at the outside desk.

The man mumbled some words into the inter-office phone. "Go on in."

"So you'd like some time off to go visit your grandmother in Provence?"

"Yes, sir." His sick grandmother in Provence had stood him in good stead several times in the past. He would be heading south just as soon as he could pick up his backpack. By the time he returned next week, it should all be over one way or another.

"Just one thing I'd like you to clear up before you go." The Commissaire fiddled with his keyboard, then turned his screen so André could see it. He turned up the volume.

"Care to explain?"

****

It was a cold, wet Tuesday morning. Nic stood shivering in the heavy rain. He'd been standing here for almost an hour now and he was soaked through. Why hadn't he thought to bring an umbrella? Because the stupid weather forecaster had said "sunny and warm." There was no place to take shelter in this courtyard in front of the Louvre. He glowered at the two lines of tourists snaking their way slowly toward the massive entrance hall under the glass pyramid.

Why weren't he and Jules waiting inside, where it was warm and dry? There was only one way in. They could have bought their tickets online and mingled with the hordes in the huge interior area under the glass. No one would have paid any attention to two more anonymous tourists. Where was Jules anyway? He was supposed to have been here an hour ago. They'd been here at opening time every day for what seemed like forever. How much longer was this going to take?

"Sorry." Jules was beside him. "The metro gets like this when it rains. The crowds are unbelievable."

Nic drew closer. "What's the plan?"

"The same as we've done every day. We watch the lines. I have a feeling about this. I think today's the day."

"I know you think she's going to try to return the

214

dragon to the Louvre. I'm not so sure. But even if she does appear, what can we do?"

"Do what you do best, Nic. No more idle threats. Use your knife. You know how to kill silently. Just do it."

"And the other two?" Nic cupped his hands, trying without success to light a cigarette in the rain. "The ones always dogging her footsteps?"

"I'll take care of them. Two hypodermics ready to go."

"You think the crowd won't be aware of three bodies collapsing in their midst?"

"Of course they will. We yell 'Help!' and 'Get a doctor!'" Jules said, exasperated. "How many times do I have to go over this with you? We search her under the pretext of helping, and disappear in the ensuing chaos with the dragon."

"It might work."

"Of course it will work."

Nic shivered. "Is there any reason we have to wait outside in the rain?"

Jules shook his head. "Just beyond that entrance with the ticket-takers is a full-blown security system, just like they have in airports. You want to get us arrested, try getting through that with your knife and my gun and hypodermics. Besides, look, the rain is stopping."

"What's that noise?" Nic looked in the direction of the bridge that crossed the Seine.

The sound of raised voices drifted toward the Louvre. Voices in unison, chanting the same words over and over. "*Jouissez sans entraves, jouissez sans entraves.*"

The booming sound bounced off the river and reverberated against the high stone walls of the Louvre as the courtyard was inundated, several hundred young people pouring into the square, carrying placards and chanting over and over again, "*Jouissez sans entraves, jouissez sans entraves.*"

"What the hell…" Jules looked angrily around him as the mob of university students surged forward, raising their fists in the air, shouting, "Free admission for all students at all times!"

He couldn't move. He was pinned in by the crush of bodies. A student pressed a placard into his hand, shouting "Join us, comrade!"

Where was Nic? Jules stretched his head, trying to see over the crush of students around him. They had to get out of here. The riot police could be arriving at any moment, and they could not afford to be caught in a general round up.

A black van pulled up behind the demonstrators. TV cameras? Reporters telecasting? How had this all happened so fast?

Shit! There was that black bastard in the front of the crowd, holding up one of the placards. It was a put-up job! The redhead must be close by. Where was he? What the hell was going on?

Police poured into the square. Jules screamed as a burly policeman yanked his arms behind him and secured them with handcuffs. "I'm not a student!" Jules protested loudly. "I'm an innocent bystander. I have nothing to do with this demonstration." He swiveled to look back at the mob. Where was Nic? Had he managed to slip away unobserved? The officer hustled him along to a waiting police van.

At the arrival of the police, the demonstrators slipped away down side streets, leaving only a few diehards still waving their placards. These the police rounded up and hauled off in waiting vans without incident.

A bored officer at the station was sitting behind his desk, registering the students rather perfunctorily. When he came to Jules, his eyes narrowed. "You're not a student."

"That's what I've been trying to say," Jules replied.

"You're Jules Allard. I remember you well." He stood half out of his chair, his hands pressed down on the desk, looming over the man in front of him threateningly. "It was me you stabbed six years ago." He sat back with a smile of smug satisfaction, and his voice hardened. "You're wanted for kidnapping and involuntary confinement of a young American woman. We should be able to hold you long enough on those charges for the extradition paperwork to go through. You're wanted for murder and arson in the U.S. Looks like you're in for the long haul this time, Jules."

****

Caitlin, Colin and Pierre Lamont sat in Pierre's black Peugeot, parked across the street from the side entrance to the Louvre. The traffic on the busy *Quai de Louvre* flowed by them.

A TV van pulled up behind them.

"I invited the television crew to join us for this," Pierre said. "Ready?"

"Aristotle was supposed to meet us here." Caitlin peered at the square, now empty of all but the reforming lines of people seeking admission to the museum. "Where is he?"

"Celine was being pushed into one of the police vans and I saw Aristotle rush to join her," Colin replied. "That wasn't supposed to happen. They were both supposed to slip away once the demonstration was under way. But he was in the front lines with Celine."

"You mean Aristotle is in jail! Again?"

"We'll see to it they are both released," Pierre said. "Once this is all over, the Director will call the Commissaire. I'm quite sure none of the demonstrators will be charged."

"It's not right. Aristotle shouldn't miss this. He's been with us from the beginning."

Colin covered her hand with his. "I know, Cait. I'm sorry. But he'll understand. Everything's set up. We have to move."

Two museum security guards approached the car, followed by a cameraman and a reporter.

Pierre said, "Are you ready?"

Caitlin took a deep breath. "Ready."

He spoke into his phone. "We're coming in now. Have the door unlocked and guards there to meet us."

For the moment, no other cars were near. Both ends of the block had been closed to traffic. Accompanied by the guards and the news team, they crossed the small stretch of pavement between the parked car and the side door to the Louvre. It opened as they approached.

With a nod to the security man there, Pierre led his small entourage through a room filled with ancient Greek and Roman sculptures to an elevator in the wide central hallway. He used a key to activate the private lift.

They exited to a large carpeted antechamber.

Caitlin didn't know what she had expected, but not this quite ordinary reception desk manned by a secretary much like one would find in any business office.

"Good morning," the young woman said. "The Director is waiting for you, Miss Abernathy, Professor Stryker, Dr. Lamont. Please go right in." Then, speaking to the news team, she added, "If you wouldn't mind waiting for a few minutes, the Director would like to speak to Miss Abernathy and her party alone first."

A distinguished-looking, silver-haired man rose from his desk as they entered. "You must be Mad'moiselle Abernathy." He walked around the desk to greet her and raised her hand to his lips. "Emile Boudin, Director of the Louvre. I have heard much about you and your two colleagues from Dr. Lamont."

Turning to Colin, he shook his hand. "Professor Stryker. I've admired your work for some years. It is good to meet you." He looked around at the assembled faces. "But there was another man involved in this, was there not?"

"Yes," Caitlin answered. "Aristotle Jones. Somehow he managed to get himself arrested in the demonstration this morning."

"Ah, yes, the demonstration. That was a fine theatrical touch. But of course you know it was nonsense. Students have been admitted free of charge to the Louvre for years."

"You know that and we know that," Caitlin smiled, "but we were pretty sure the likes of Nic Bisset and Jules Allard wouldn't know that."

"I understand you were put at considerable risk over this venture," the Director said. "You were kidnapped and injured, and might be dead had it not been for the efforts of your two colleagues."

"Yet here I am," Caitlin answered, smiling.

"Yes, here you are. And you look well-recovered from your experiences." He walked back around the desk to sit in his deep leather chair. "Now, if you are ready, Miss Abernathy, I should like to see the amulet. It was a particular favorite of mine. We have more valuable pieces in the collection, of course, but few so beautifully worked."

Caitlin took the silk jewelry pouch out of her purse and unwrapped it on the desk. She withdrew the silver dolphin and polished it with the silk until it gleamed. Then, taking it gently in both hands, she opened it and placed it on the desk to show its contents. The dragon lay there in its silver casket, its rubies glowing as if on fire, its pearl luminescent, its aura spellbinding. She touched it, knowing this would be the last time she could ever do so.

There was silence in the room.

The Director took a deep breath. "I suppose it's time to allow the media in. Close the case so you can open the dolphin again for them as you did for me. What a brilliant way to have transported it! I have champagne chilling. We'll drink a toast to the return of Marie Antoinette's amulet, for the benefit of the evening news."

****

Nic was fuming. He'd been trying to find a dry spot in which to light his cigarette when he saw the policeman clamping the cuffs on Jules. For the first time in his life, he was grateful for his short stature. He'd been able to weave his way unnoticed through the fleeing students. Now what? Jules was in the hands of

220

the police and was unlikely to be able to talk his way out. It was all because of that damned woman, that interfering American *putain*. It was her fault Jules was now in police hands. He couldn't do anything to save Jules but he could make the bitch pay.

Could he even return to his flat safely? Perhaps if he moved quickly enough. He'd need the money they had hidden there and his favorite knife for this very special job.

But where were they staying? They'd checked out of the hotel he'd been watching and just disappeared.

The demonstration...there had been a truck there from one of the TV stations. And newspaper reporters. The whole episode would be on the six o'clock news.

He reached into his pocket for his phone and a brochure for the Louvre fell to the floor. He'd forgotten he had it. He'd absently picked it up off the ground when they were doing their surveillance there. There was a contact number.

He punched in the numbers and was surprised when he was answered almost immediately.

"The Louvre. How may I direct your call?"

"The office of the director, please."

A short pause, the number ringing.

"This is the office of the Director. Marie Maynard, Administrative Assistant to the Director speaking. How may I help you?"

He was silent for a moment, thinking faster than he ever had in his life

The woman at the other end of the line repeated her question, "Hello? How may I help you?"

He smoothed out his speech, to make more like that of the woman on the other end of the line.

"I'm so sorry to disturb you with my problem," he said, "But I'm a reporter with Le Figaro, and I need to verify some information with Dr. Stryker in time for tonight's edition. Have you any way I can reach him? An address, perhaps?"

"I'm sure I have the address where he's staying here someplace…ah, yes, here it is. It's in the Marais."

Nic wrote the address down carefully and thanked the woman for her help.

Chapter Eighteen

"I can't believe it's over." Closing the apartment door behind them, Caitlin sighed and kicked off her shoes. She turned to Colin, twined her hands around his neck, and brought his lips down to hers. "Ummm…"

She broke away, breathless. "But I still haven't seen Paris. We've been in France ten days and I haven't seen Paris."

"I thought you would want to get home as soon as possible once the dragon was returned. I know you've been worried about that commission, so I booked our tickets for day after tomorrow."

Caitlin made a face. "Marcus-Pfeiffer. I'd almost forgotten. It seems years ago."

"But that still gives us tonight and all day tomorrow. What would you like to do?"

"Everything. We never got to the Musee d'Orsay. I want to see Notre Dame and Sacre Coeur. I want to watch the painters working on the sidewalks in Montmartre. I want to see the inside of that wonderful, wedding cake opera house, the Garnier, is it? I want to go shopping. What girl doesn't want silk underwear from Paris!"

"I think that might all be doable in a day. I can get us tickets to the Garnier for tonight. Shall I see if Aristotle and Celine want to join us?"

As if on cue, Aristotle walked in. "Sorry we missed

the big moment, guys, but we caught it later on TV. There wasn't any problem with getting released, but it took some time. And I couldn't leave Celine on her own."

"Where is Celine now?" Colin asked.

"She went to see her mother. They have a lot to talk about."

"So what's with you and Celine?" Caitlin teased.

Aristotle shrugged. "She's a nice girl. I like her."

"Like her?" Caitlin teased.

Aristotle chose to ignore the innuendo. "More than like her. So what's up?"

"We're going to a performance at the Garnier," Caitlin said.

Aristotle frowned. "Are you sure that's wise? Nic Bisset is still out there somewhere."

"He won't have stayed in Paris after Allard's capture," Colin assured him. "It wouldn't make sense. My guess is he'll have put as many miles as possible between himself and the Paris police. We'll take precautions, but I think we can feel free to see a little of Paris before we get on a plane day after tomorrow."

"I guess so." Aristotle still looked doubtful. "So where are you going? The Garnier? What's that?"

"It's the old opera house, built in the 1800s. For a performance of the ballet." Caitlin said. "Why don't you and Celine come with us?"

"Ballet? I don't think so. Celine and I were going to hit a few clubs she knows, later, when she comes home. "

"Tomorrow then? It's our last day here and we're going on a sightseeing whirlwind."

"Sure. Where shall we meet you?"

Caitlin turned to Colin.

"Sacré-Coeur, I think," he answered. "It's in the heart of Montmartre, on the top of the highest hill in Paris. With an uncountable number of steps straight up from the bottom of the hill, if you want to climb them. Caitlin likes climbing steps. We're planning to be there for sunrise at seven. I remember from my student days, the views over Paris at that hour are spectacular. We'll meet you right in front of the basilica at the top of the steps. "

"Okay. We may not make it back home tonight, but we'll meet you at Sacré-Coeur at sunrise tomorrow morning."

****

Caitlin looked around her at the tier upon tier of gilded boxes with red velvet drapes and pretty, if uncomfortable, chairs in the Opera Garnier. She could see only about half the stage from their very expensive box on the first tier. The dancers whirling below her in a production of *Giselle* brought to mind the wonderful Degas paintings of dancers she so loved. It seemed that in the hundred years since Degas, nothing had changed here.

"Why do people pay so much money for seats where they can't even see the whole stage?" she whispered to Colin.

"Back when this house was built, it wasn't about seeing," he answered. "It was about being seen. Have you had enough? We can leave at the intermission."

Caitlin glanced around the ornate, beautiful theater, and at the dancers whirling on the stage below, and nodded. "Yes. Enough. Let's go walk in the rain and get something to eat."

A half hour later they crossed the rain-streaked square to the Café de la Paix. A black-coated waiter hovered over them.

"We'd just like a dessert and a coffee, please. You choose for us," Colin instructed.

Caitlin squealed with delight at the confection in front of her. A baked apple encased in chocolate, complete with a little green pastry leaf. She took a bite. It tasted as good as it looked. Colin pronounced his more common crème brulée quite acceptable. Caitlin offered Colin a bite of her treat and watched as he savored it. She reached across the table and licked a drop of chocolate off his lips.

"I think we need to get back to the apartment. Now," he said. Pulling her to her feet, he threw some euros on the table and led her out to the closest taxi stand. He gave the address to the driver, then pulled her to him. His hands were everywhere, his kisses hot with desire.

Caitlin squirmed, conscious of the smiling cab driver, but too aroused to care.

They made it back to the Marais, clothes in disarray. Colin pushed Caitlin unceremoniously into the now-working lift. As the elevator made its ponderous way up to the fifth floor, Colin pushed her against the wall and slid her skirt up to her waist, breathing heavily. She shuddered and moaned as the door of the lift slid open at the fifth floor.

He scooped her up in his arms and with one shaking hand managed to unlock the door, slam it behind them, and push her down on the bed. Without even pausing to undress he knelt over her, his breathing labored, his eyes dazed. Caitlin was making inarticulate sounds of wanting, wriggled, unable to lie still.

****

On the street below Nic watched as the cab discharged two passengers who were clearly unaware of anything but each other. It would be so easy to take them in the moment, to kill them both before they reached the door. He fingered his knife. No. He wanted to kill by the light of day. Just the woman. He wanted the man to watch him kill the woman, to know loss as he was feeling loss. He and Jules had been together for thirty years. How could he go on without Jules? Tears blinded him.

****

The next morning the small alarm on Colin's phone awakened him at six. He looked down at Caitlin, sleeping deeply beside him, her hair disordered on the pillow, her warm nude rump pressed against him. He hated to awaken her. They had made love again during the night. He was sure she was exhausted. Strangely, he was not. He felt only exhilaration. The knowledge that he could bring her to blind passion so easily again and again was heady. He could feel the warning hardening even now as he looked at her. Would he ever have enough of her? He hoped not.

But today he had promised to show her Paris. He leaned over and pushed her hair back from her face. "Wake up, sleepyhead. We have a busy day today."

She mumbled, "Go away."

"Up, Caitlin!" He pulled the covers off her.

"Mrphh."

Colin looked down at the determinedly sleeping figure on the bed and frowned. She would regret it if she didn't go sightseeing today. Tomorrow, when they were on a plane heading back to California, she would be sorry.

Without thinking further, he picked her up and headed for the shower. She nestled trustingly against him. In the shower, still holding her, he turned the water on, full force. He hadn't intended the water to be icy.

She screamed, now fully awake, battering him with her fists. "You beast! Put me down!"

"Sorry about that. I forgot how long it takes to get the hot water up to this bathroom. But now that I have your attention, we have a date with Celine and Aristotle at Sacre-Coeur at sunrise. That's about forty-five minutes from now."

"We do, don't we? Somehow in the last eight hours I forgot there was any life beyond sex." She reached down and caressed him, bringing him instantly to hard arousal.

He growled and reached to pull her to him.

She laughed and slipped out of his grasp. "Get dressed, Colin. The bed will be there later."

"How do you expect me to get pants over this? Come on, Caitlin, five minutes..."

"No. We're going sight-seeing. I've heard abstinence is good for you. We'll try it for the next twenty-four hours."

"Twenty-four..."

"Get dressed or it might be forty-eight hours."

"Aristophanes," he grumbled.

"What?" Caitlin had struggled into her jeans and was now pulling a sweater on over her head.

Colin followed suit. Jeans, T-shirt, sweater. "An ancient Greek playwright. He wrote a play in which the

228

women control history by withholding sex from their men. It has kept audiences laughing for over two thousand years. You ready?"

"I think I'd like to see that play. Do we need jackets?"

"Definitely. It's a chilly twelve degrees out there. Celsius that is."

****

Aristotle and Celine had danced the night away. At five in the morning, surrounded by market workers, they ate onion soup, rich beef stock thick with onions and bread and melted cheese.

Now they sat on the top of the steps at Sacré-Coeur as the night gently faded into day. They huddled together under a blanket Celine had the foresight to bring.

Aristotle wished he could keep the sun from rising, hold back the day when he would have to leave Celine.

"We return to Berkeley tomorrow."

"I know."

They sat in silence for a few minutes.

Aristotle had never thought it could happen to him. Falling in love was for other people. But here he was, so much in love he could hardly think straight.

He pushed the words out quickly, afraid to hear her answer. "Come with me, Celine. I can't offer you much at this point, but I'll have my doctorate within a year, and hopefully there'll be an academic appointment after that. It's not a bad life, the life of an academic."

Celine turned and touched his face, gently. "I want nothing more than to be with you, Aristotle. I wish I could come with you now. But I don't feel I can leave my mother at this point. She needs me. She has finally agreed to see a doctor. Perhaps in a few months…"

He felt a surge of happiness. She hadn't said no. "A few months is good. Meanwhile I'll ratchet up the pace of my work. With no real need, I've kind of drifted. But if I know you'll come…"

"I promise I'll come as soon as I can."

Aristotle gave a sigh of content and pulled her closer. The city below them took on a warm rosy glow. "Caitlin and Colin are going to miss the sunrise if they don't get here soon."

"Isn't that them? Climbing the hill?"

Aristotle peered at the two figures still only halfway up the steps from the bottom of the hill, far below. "It's them, all right. Caitlin has this crazy thing about steps."

They watched as Caitlin ran merrily up the steps, Colin straggling behind her, trying to catch up. They could hear her laughter pealing in the early morning quiet.

Caitlin had almost reached them when Aristotle sensed rather than saw a figure running out of the shadows, heading for Caitlin.

As the phantom reached the place where he and Celine sat huddled together, Aristotle stretched out his long legs into the path of the running man. He didn't think about it, he acted instinctively.

The man tripped and stumbled, then rolled over and over down the length of the stairway leading from the Basilica. His knife flew out of his hand, clattering to fall at Caitlin's feet. At the landing, his body came to rest, his head at an impossible angle.

Caitlin screamed as Colin reached her and pulled her away from the body of Nic Bisset.

Chapter Nineteen

It was three days before they were finally able to board a flight for home. The police were sympathetic, but formalities had to be observed, even if the dead man was known as a hardened criminal.

"He tripped and fell?"

"Yes." They all agreed that was what had happened.

"You were very fortunate. He was up to no good, with that knife in his possession."

They all agreed they were, indeed, very fortunate.

****

Caitlin was weary in mind and body as the tired trio staggered through customs and immigration at the San Francisco airport and made their way to an airport van. In Berkeley, they were the last passengers to be discharged, Aristotle at his apartment over the shop, then Caitlin at her hilltop home. Colin gave the driver the address of his apartment near the university.

Back home in this house she had always loved, Caitlin stood just inside her front door and looked around. It seemed so empty without Colin. For some reason she was near tears. She hadn't expected him to leave her so abruptly. He hadn't even kissed her in parting.

She had assumed he would come in with her, stay here with her in her house. It had never occurred to her that they wouldn't be together the way they had been all the weeks before they went to Paris, and the weeks they were in France. She had become accustomed to having him around, laughing with her, talking with her, cooking scrumptious meals for her, holding her, making love to her.

She took a deep breath, picked up her bag and went up the stairs to her room. If that's the way it was going to be, she'd better get used to it. She'd been alone before. She knew how to survive alone. In less than a month, Colin Stryker would be returning to Ireland, to his job and his family. He would probably find someone there to share his bed.

She had her work. It had always been the solution to all her problems. She could lose herself in her work.

Then why did she feel as if her world was crumbling around her? She threw herself down on her bed and gave in to the tears burning behind her eyes. She sobbed herself to sleep.

****

The next day, at five in the afternoon, her doorbell rang. Colin stood there, a bunch of daisies in one hand and a grocery bag in the other.

"I brought dinner. I was pretty sure there wouldn't be anything in the house to eat."

Caitlin burst into tears.

"What…Caitlin, what's wrong?"

"I thought—oh, never mind what I thought. You're here."

They cooked together, Caitlin doing all the chopping and setting the table while Colin attended to the more serious side of the culinary art. At seven, they sat down to a delicious, candle-lit dinner with wine.

How could she have been so wrong? He wanted to be here, with her. Everything was right with her world once again.

After dinner, they adjourned to the living room. They sat on the torn sofa cushions on the floor as they had all those weeks before Paris, Colin's arm around her shoulder, her head on his shoulder, soft jazz playing on the radio.

"I'll be going back to Ireland soon."

Caitlin held her breath and waited for him to ask. He had to ask her to come with him. What would her answer be? He couldn't expect her to uproot herself from everything she knew. Her home, her career. Her life was here. Still she waited for him to speak, to ask her.

"It's getting late, Cait. I must go. I have an important meeting in the morning." He stood and extended his hand to her, pulling her to her feet.

He wasn't going to stay with her for the night? She followed him to the door. There he reached down and kissed her lightly on the nose. "Goodnight, Caitlin. I'll call you."

He was out the door and gone before she could react.

He would *call her*? Fuming, Catlin picked up the nearest thing she could put her hands on, a Chinese vase, and hurled it at the fireplace.

Then she sat down on the floor and cried. That vase had been one of her mother's favorites. What was the matter with her? He had her so out of control she didn't know what she was doing.

It was three days before she next heard from him. He once again appeared unannounced at her front door, flowers in one hand, grocery bag in the other.

She almost slammed the door in his face.

"What's wrong, Cait? I thought I'd make dinner for us. Did you have other plans? I should have called, but I've been busy."

Through gritted teeth, Caitlin answered, "No. No other plans. By all means make dinner."

Her anger subsided over tournedos Rossini and apple flan. Once again they adjourned to the living room and sat on the floor. Caitlin didn't want conversation. She wanted him in her bed. It had been a week now and she was suffering mightily from withdrawal. How could he be so cool and collected? She'd fix that.

She pulled him to her and kissed him with every ounce of guile she knew. Her tongue twined with his, her hands splayed against his chest. He tasted so wonderful, wine and apples and male, all male. She slid her hands down his body. Oh, yes, he was ready. He was more than ready.

Colin broke off the kiss and stood up. He straightened his clothes. "Sorry, Cait. I have to go home. Early day tomorrow."

He was gone before she had a chance to react.

What the hell?

****

The next day she confided in Aristotle. "I thought he loved me. He won't touch me. He's tender and kind, but we haven't made love since we got home. What's wrong, Aristotle? I can't go on like this."

"What would you do if he asked you to come to Ireland with him? Have you thought about that?"

"Yes. Of course I've thought about it. I think about

it constantly. I don't know what I'd do. I don't know whether I can leave my work and my home here. I don't know if I could ever be just the professor's wife."

"Why do you think Colin would even want you to be 'just the professor's wife'? From what I know of him, that's the last thing he'd want. He loves you for who you are, a beautiful and intelligent young woman and a brilliant designer of jewelry with an important career ahead of you. He'd never expect you to give that up to be 'just the professor's wife.' But make no mistake—he wants a real life with you, a loving home, children, the whole ball game. Are you ready for that? That's the conversation you should be having with him. Don't be swayed by the example of your parents' marriage, Cait. Not all marriages fail. My parents were happily married for fifty years."

"I do want marriage. I want a home and children. I never thought I would, but I do. I want Colin's children. But you're missing the point here, Aristotle. It's not just about whether I'm willing to give up my life here and move to Ireland with him. We've been home for two weeks and he'll be leaving soon and"—tears welled up—"and he hasn't asked me to come to with him. He hasn't even hinted at marriage, or a possible future for us." She dabbed at her eyes with Aristotle's proffered red handkerchief. "And he hasn't even made love to me, not once."

"Maybe he doesn't want your decision clouded by sex. Or," Aristotle smiled, "Maybe he's playing another game altogether. You said he once mentioned a Greek play, Lysistrata."

"What? The one where all the women of Athens withhold sex to get their men to do what they want?"

"Think about it, Caitlin. It makes sense in a crazy kind of way. What does Colin want? You. What do you want? At this moment, apparently, sex. Ergo, you will get what you want if you give Colin what he wants."

"You're crazy. What does he want that I'm not willing to give him?"

Aristotle took Caitlin's hands in his. "Perhaps commitment?"

****

Caitlin thought about what Aristotle had said as she drove home. He was right. It wasn't about sex, it was about commitment, on both sides. She loved Colin and she was pretty sure he loved her. Marriage and children? She had always imagined that someday in the far distant future she would marry and have children. But now that "someday" loomed in front of her she was just plain scared. Could she be a loving wife and a good mother to the children they might have? She wasn't sure. Her parent's marriage hadn't offered her much of a model. But she did love Colin, and he came from a large and loving family. He would make a good father. They could work something out. They just needed to sit down and talk about it.

Then, infuriatingly, he didn't call or come by for an entire week. In desperation, she called the University.

"I'm sorry," a cold female voice answered. "Dr. Stryker is in Ireland at the moment."

Caitlin swallowed her rising panic. "When are you expecting him back?"

"I really couldn't say. He didn't leave that information with us. I could put a note on his desk. Who shall I say called?"

"Never mind." Caitlin hung up. He was gone. Gone

236

without saying good-bye. Could what they had have meant so little to him?

The week went by with agonizing slowness. Caitlin pushed herself out of bed each morning and forced herself to go to the shop, to work. Forced herself to go home each evening, to eat a lonely meal, then to bed for another sleepless night. The last of the Marcus-Pfeiffer order was completed and sent off. She was at loose ends. She had always been able to lose herself in her work, but now she was unable to concentrate even on that.

She decided to swallow her pride. When Colin came back, if Colin came back, if he asked her, she would go with him to Ireland. She couldn't go on like this. Life wasn't worth living.

But what if he didn't come back? What if he didn't ask her? She stiffened her back. Well then, she'd just have to go to Ireland after him. This was the twenty-first century. A woman didn't have to wait to be asked.

Once she had made her decision, she slept better. She would wait until she was sure he wasn't returning, and then she would go to Ireland and confront him. Was her serious about her or had she been just another fling?

On the last day of the month, her doorbell rang. Colin was there, flowers in one hand, a grocery bag in the other.

Caitlin burst into tears and slammed the door in his face. Then she opened it again to find him still standing there, a puzzled look on his face.

"What's wrong, Caitlin? Have I done something to offend you?"

The look of injured innocence on his face drove

Caitlin wild. "Done anything wrong? You haven't done anything right since we got home. You haven't told me what's going on in your life. You went back to Ireland without telling me. You haven't"—Caitlin stumbled over the words, sniffling—"you haven't made love to me since we got back."

"Let me in, Cait, so we can talk."

She stepped back so he could come into the house. She followed him through to the kitchen, where he arranged the flowers in a vase and stowed the groceries in the fridge.

"Okay, Caitlin," he said, pulling out a kitchen chair to sit facing her. "I'm here. Was there something you wanted to tell me?"

She took a deep breath. "I'll come to Ireland with you."

"I don't recall asking you to come to Ireland with me. In fact I may not be going back to Ireland any time soon."

Confusion covered her. What was he saying?

"I've been offered a Chair at U.C. Berkeley."

"A chair?" she sniffled. "For heaven's sake, do you mean your office didn't have a chair?"

"Not a chair to sit on, Caitlin, a capital 'C' Chair!"

Caitlin hadn't the foggiest idea what he was talking about.

"It's like this, Caitlin, in academia, there are ranks: assistant professor, associate professor, full professor. It takes years to progress through those ranks. At each stage, one has to meet certain criteria, evidence of scholarship, writing, research and teaching. I, of course, went through them all rather quickly. I'm a tenured full professor."

Caitlin nodded. Of course, he would have risen through the ranks. He was brilliant and Aristotle had told her about his international reputation. She waited.

"But this named, *endowed* Chair, is above and beyond all those ranks. It brings with it a higher income, more time for research and a guaranteed position for life. And, I might add, quite a bit of prestige."

She could hardly believe what she was hearing. "So you're going to accept this Chair? You're going to stay here in Berkeley?"

"I haven't decided yet. It's a long way from all my family. I have no one here."

Caitlin hesitated. Then in a small voice she said, "You have me."

"Do I, Caitlin? Do I have you? You could find someone else tomorrow, and then where would I be?"

"But I don't want anyone else."

"That's today, Caitlin. I would have an endowed chair from the university, but to stay here, I'm afraid I need an *endowed bed* from you. I need some assurance that you won't change your mind. Like tenure at the university."

"But that's silly. I won't change my mind. And how can I offer you an endowed bed?" She hesitated. "Of course I could always marry you. Would that be *endowed* enough for you?"

Colin paused as if in thought. "Hmm. I hadn't considered marriage. *With all my worldly goods I thee endow.* Yes, I think that might be endowed enough to keep me here. We'll have to act quickly, though. I've promised to give the university my answer within three weeks."

"Three weeks? I'm supposed to plan a wedding in three weeks?"

"I'm sure we can do it. Aristotle already has the job well in hand. He has the guest list drawn up and he's booked Friday, three weeks from today, at four pm for us at St. Timothy's."

"You beast! You planned this whole thing!" Caitlin pummeled his chest with her fists. "You tricked me!"

Colin laughed, and grabbed her hands in his. He kissed her deeply. When they came up for breath, he said, "I needed to give you time to think, Caitlin. To be sure you wanted what I want. Marriage, a real life together, family. Are you sure that's what you want? I'm talking lifetime commitment, Caitlin, no going back."

Caitlin sighed and nestled into his arms. "Yes. A lifetime commitment. *Until death us do part.* That's what I want." She pushed herself out of his arms. "Wait a minute. You're talking about a wedding three weeks from today! I need to go shopping for a wedding dress. And I need to see Aristotle's list. What about your family? Tante Adéle, Oncle Bertrand, your mother? I haven't even met your mother. Suppose she doesn't like me?"

"I've already told them. And my mother will love you. They're all arriving on the Wednesday before the wedding."

"Were you so very sure I'd ask you to marry me?"

"No. But if you hadn't, I'd have told you about the church and the date and I'd have got you there somehow, if I'd had to drag you there bodily, like Petruchio dragged his Kate in *The Taming of the Shrew.* I love you, Cait, and you love me, and we belong together. *Come on and kiss me, Cait.*"

Caitlin moved into his arms where she belonged, and always would belong, and gave a contented sigh.

A word about the author...

Blair McDowell's first career was as a musician and teacher. She studied in Europe and, during the course of her academic career, lived in Hungary, the United States, Australia, and Canada, teaching in universities in the latter three countries. She has always loved to write and has produced six widely used professional books and numerous articles in her field.

A voracious reader, Blair decided when she retired from university teaching to turn her talents to her first love, writing fiction. She moved to Canada's scenic west coast and, with a friend, opened a bed & breakfast. Mornings she makes omelets and chats with guests from far and near, and afternoons, she writes. From March through September, the world comes to her doorstep, bringing tales that are fodder for her rich imagination, but once the tourist season is over, she packs her bags and takes off for exotic ports—Europe in the fall, the Caribbean in the winter.

http://www.blairmcdowell.com

CPSIA information can be obtained
at www.ICGtesting.com
Printed in the USA
LVOW03s2107140817
545016LV00013B/117/P